For Judy

Oh, God!

1

I HAVE to tell you right off that I don't love first-person narratives. I always figure the writer is trying to save himself work if he has his main character tell the story. I love it even less if the work is autobiographical and he uses first person, because then you have to sit through all those I's. So that's the way I feel. A writer who can't use a metaphor to tell his story is lazy and I thought I'd get that out of the way in the very first paragraph, even though I'm going to tell this in the first person myself.

I have no choice, really. I couldn't make believe this was about somebody else and still have it stand as The Official Version of what happened. Also, to be completely open about it, I need to do this. The telling of this is about the only thing I'm qualified to do right now. Maybe when this book is out I can make a little career out of discussing it, but with the way I've overstayed my welcome with the media, I kind of doubt it.

How I ever qualified to get involved in the first place is up for speculation. I'd like to think it was because I had demonstrated a writing and reporting talent and was not yet tainted by success. Not yet tainted by success!—the refuge of every struggling writer. But I suppose I was Everyman. Or more specifically, Everywriterman. I almost didn't get that far. From time to time I considered giving up writing for a living and becoming . . . I didn't know what. I found myself actually reading vocational guidance posters in subways and buses.

"Could You Be Earning More Money $$$$ If You Went to a Technical School?" I was sure I could. "Be a Transit Authority Policeman." I was too old. "Join the Peace Corps." For that, my wife, Judy, would have had to leave her job, something she wasn't quite ready to do, and for which she earned $12,000 last year, compared to my $5,500 free-lancing, and that in itself could make a person wonder—could you be earning more money $$$$ if you went to a technical school?

With all this about money, I must point out that I

was at heart a creative artist, a playwright with two full-length plays written, but unfortunately no producer or director had shown enough interest in them, and my play agent, a lady whom I could never reach on the phone, had said, "Don't worry—that kind of play will come back," whatever that meant.

Meantime, I found I could pick up rent money doing interviews with show-business personalities and selling them to places like the Sunday *Times* or the *Ladies' Home Journal*. Then I did a piece about a Rolling Stones press conference. It was the kind of typical scene that rock superstars generate—lights, cameras, fans, the press climbing all over each other, silly questions and cute answers. The Stones, performers that they are, went through a performance. So I reviewed the performance. It was printed in the *Times*, and even though I felt it was just a straight job of reporting, people started talking about it as "the definitive capsulization of the rock music scene" and words to that effect. It made a big splash, and suddenly I was known as the guy who did the piece on The Stones' press conference.

Because of the article, I found myself on all kinds of mailing lists I didn't want to be on, and there were endless invitations arriving at the house—press parties for singing groups, cocktail parties for celebrities, luncheons for authors, and these, combined with letters for Judy, department store announcements, and our regular monthly bills—you had to be a copy editor just to do the mail.

This particular morning, Judy had dropped a bundle of mail on me in bed, where I still was, a point of contention in our house where the executive wife goes off to work while the husband stays at home, but I had to sleep late that morning—I was up for hours during the night, lying there recalling large passages from memory of my "Collected Works." What had triggered this was seeing a college girl on the subway the day before underlining sections of a book she was studying with a red pen, and thinking, Now that's class; will I ever in my life write anything a person would actually underline?

I started to go through the mail and in among the junk was an envelope addressed to me with no return address. Inside was a sheet of plain white bond paper and typed on an electric typewriter it said:

```
God grants you an interview. Go to 600
Madison Avenue, room 3700, Monday, at
11 a.m.
```

My first thought was that it was a press agent's stunt. Or maybe it was a teaser mailing. Or a prank. It couldn't be God. God was God! Also I was brought up on something called *Bible Comics*, true-to-life adventures of biblical heroes, and there were wonderful things like David and Goliath, and God and Moses, and God was always pretty impressive, talking from the heavens or booming down His voice from mountaintops, all of which made an early impression on me—so the idea of a typed letter from an Executive God didn't make much sense. There was even a typo in the "v" in Avenue. Just a little mistake, but a mistake nonetheless, only I couldn't begin to deal with the possible metaphysical implications of that.

But what was it? It was a gimmick—a Florida land scheme and they get you up there and show you a movie of condominiums in "paradise." It was a nut—he gets you up there and undresses.

I called Judy for an opinion, but she was out of the office somewhere. So it was up to me. "God" was granting me an interview at 11 A.M. and it was already 10. I just didn't know what to make of it. There was something peculiar about it. No press agent or businessman would send out an invitation like that with such little information in it. Only somebody very crazy or very dumb—or very sure of himself. Could it possibly *be* God? It couldn't. But if it were God, it could have been God. God can do anything. A line that John Updike once wrote flashed across my mind, about Ted Williams not acknowledging the Boston fans in his last game. He wrote, "Gods do not answer letters." But I couldn't remember anybody ever saying anything about their sending them.

Well, whoever it was had done a job on me. I was curious. No, that's too casual. Deep down I must have hoped, it *is* God. It's this incredible miracle and I'm in on it.

13

And what if it were this incredible thing? What if God *had* chosen me? How would I deal with it? What could I possibly say to Him? Like most people, I had wondered about God and the Universe and The Nature of Things. But I wasn't a theological scholar. Apart from those *Bible Comics* and Hebrew School, which I almost flunked, the deepest I ever went on God was in late-night discussions with girls I was trying to seduce after seeing Ingmar Bergman movies.

I didn't know what to do. Miracles don't happen—except when they happen—*if* they happen. I went through a truly baroque reasoning process and finally came up with—Go. If it's a stunt maybe you'll get a story out of it, and if it's *real*, try not to think about it. It's called confronting a dilemma sideways.

On the bus uptown, I began feeling alternately foolish about going and apprehensive about what I was getting into. By the time I reached 600 Madison, I was in a totally confused state, deterred momentarily by the sight of a U.S. mail truck with a poster on the side, "Join the Modern Coast Guard," and thinking maybe I should have.

I took the elevator to the 37th floor and followed an arrow which pointed to room 3700. There was no name on the door, just the numerals "3700." I knocked, waited, and then tried the door. It was open and I went in. The office was empty except for a chair and an intercom machine on the floor.

Then from the intercom there came this voice. It

was *His* voice! Yes, Himself Himself. The voice wasn't booming and spectacular. It was just a voice, a little weary, a little whiny actually—and God's first words to me were:

"Listen, I like the piece you did on The Rolling Stones."

"Who are you? What is this?"

"I'm God."

"This is crazy."

"Be nice," He said.

"You're God?"

It couldn't be, I thought.

"It is," He said.

"How can you be God? You're a voice on an intercom."

"Well, you're not allowed to see me."

"Why not?"

"Because."

"It's just not possible."

"It's possible."

"Prove it. Prove you're God."

"I don't do proof," He said.

"I'm getting out of here."

"Wait. Where are you?"

"Room 3700, 600 Madison Avenue."

"So you know what? In this building, there is no room 3700."

I got out of there. A person can take just so much weirdness. I took the elevator down to the lobby and looked around. The sign over the elevator said "12—26." The other one said "2—11." I was sure I had seen something when I first came in that said "12—37." I asked the elevator starter how did I get to 3700 and he said there is no 3700 and I almost fainted.

I was tempted to leave then and there, but I couldn't. I went back in the elevator, pressed the button for 26, and when the elevator stopped, I was facing a sign that said "37th floor." I walked down the hall, opened the door to 3700 and the voice said:

"So stop with this riding up and down."

I want to tell you I was pretty scared.

"Don't be scared," He said. "I went to a lot of trouble so you wouldn't be."

"What is this?"

"What this is—is an interview. I am God and you are you, and I'm giving you an exclusive."

"You can't be God."

"You know this for a fact?"

"God wouldn't do this. He wouldn't invite someone to a strange room like this."

"You know what your trouble is?"

"I'm hallucinating—that's my trouble."

"You've read too many *Bible Comics*."

"If you're God"—imagine saying that to God—"if you're God, then why all this? Why didn't you just appear over my bed?"

"Because you'd get too frightened. You'd probably jump out the window."

"If you're God, how come you've got such a thin little voice? If you're God, how come you talk a little whiny, a little like my Uncle Simon?"

"Empathy," He said.

"What?"

"What I'm doing. I'm talking to you in a way you can accept. I'm relating."

"Relating?"

"Well, I don't want to brag, but if I appeared to you just as God, your mind couldn't grasp it."

My mind wasn't doing such a good job as it was.

"And the letter and this meeting . . ."

"To bring you along gradually. So you can cope."

"Well, I don't believe any of this."

"That's the whole problem. That's why I decided to show up. Too many nonbelievers."

I was bewildered.

"Come on. Be a good reporter. This is the biggest story of your life."

"I think you should talk to James Reston."

"No. You're the fella. That piece on The Stones. I liked it a lot. Peppy. Today you need peppy in order to communicate—and I want to communicate."

What I said next was—"Why?" I guess what was working on me was some residual belief that there *is* a God and it *could* be God—and if it *is* God, you go along with Him, don't you? He's God! So I asked, "Why?" and right there, I was into it. God had finessed me into an interview.

2

"I'LL TELL you why I'm doing this," He said. "They've been going around saying I'm dead or worse."

"What's worse?"

"That I never was, or what I was was gas or *shmutz*."

"*Shmutz?*"

"You know, particles. With the big bang theories and the little bang theories. When you're God, it's insulting."

He was confiding in me!

18

"Let's stop right here. I really think you should be talking to somebody higher up. The Pope maybe."

"No, I looked into this. And you're my fella."

I'm His fella! What if I don't ask the right questions? What if I misquote Him? A misquote here has cosmic significance.

"Excuse me. What do I call you?"

"Call me God."

"God, I think I should have a tape recorder."

"Forget it. It wouldn't work."

"Why?"

"My voice—it wouldn't come out on the tape."

"I don't understand."

"I can't go into it. It's very complex. It's like . . . what would you understand? Ghosts. You know how they used to say a ghost was not supposed to cast a shadow? Well, it's like that. You can't record God's voice."

"I really don't understand."

"*Oy-oy-oy*," He said. "Because it's not my real voice. I'm just making this up for you, so you can hear it. I mean, I'm God over everybody, but I'm not speaking Chinese, am I?"

"Actually you sound a little Jewish."

"What then? You're a little Jewish, aren't you?"

"Yes."

"So like I'm telling you, I'm doing this for you. By the way, I was at your Bar Mitzvah. It didn't knock me out."

"You were there?"

"I'm there for everything—prayers, weddings, Bar Mitzvahs, funerals, baptisms—you name it. 'The Pledge of Allegiance' to the flag with that *under God* thing in it—I'm there. A fella stubs his toe and says 'goddammit' —I'm there. Kate Smith sings 'God Bless America'—I'm there."

"For everything? Everywhere on earth, any time anyone invokes the name of God . . . ?"

"I'm there. I got to cover a lot of territory in my work."

"That's an incredible concept. That's something Man has wanted to know for centuries. Are prayers heard? Does God listen?"

"Who says I listen? I only said I'm there. After a while, who can listen?"

"Then God *doesn't* care."

"I care. I care plenty. But what can I do?"

"But you're God!"

"Only for The Big Picture."

"What?"

"I don't get into details."

"Why?"

"It's better that I shouldn't meddle. What am I going to do—get into favorites? So I come up with the concepts, the big ideas—the details can take care of themselves."

"Then the way things happen on earth . . ."

"They happen. Don't look at me."

20

"And there's no plan, no scheme that controls our destinies?"

"A lot of it is luck. Luck and who you know."

I was staggered. He just went zipping along.

"Looking back, of course I made a few mistakes. Giraffes. It was a good thought, but it really didn't work out. Avocados—on that I made the pit too big. Then there are things that worked pretty good. Photosynthesis is a big favorite of mine. Spring is nice. Tomatoes are cute. Also raccoons."

"But what about *Man?*" I was trying to rise to the responsibility. "What about his future? The future of the planet?"

"It's a good question."

"And?"

"I couldn't tell you."

"Don't you know?"

"Well, like I say, I don't get into that. Of course I hope you make it. I mean, I'm a real fan. But it's like in a ball game. If you're in the stands, you can root, but that's about all."

"You're God. You can protect our future, alleviate suffering, work miracles!"

"I don't do miracles. They're too flashy and they upset the natural balance. Oh, maybe I'll do a miracle now and then, just for fun—if it's not too important. The last miracle I did was the 1969 Mets and before that the 1914 Boston Braves and before that I think you have to go back to the Red Sea."

"But, as God, you have the power to intervene, to help us in emergencies."

"So where do I draw the line? Say a fella is going to eat a hamburger that's not 100 percent beef. What do I do, knock it out of his hand? How would you like to live with Divine Hands popping out of the sky all the time? It would make people crazy."

"But I'm talking about wars and poverty and health. That's not on the level of hamburgers."

"That depends on where you sit."

"So you've decided to just let us stumble along, and never do a thing to help?"

"You got to understand, I went through my manipulative, controlling stage. You know what I mean from manipulative? It was back in the Ten Commandments days. Now I had it in mind there should be about five thousand commandments, to cover every eventuality. Things like: Thou Shalt Pick Up the Trash from the Picnic Areas. Thou Shalt Help Old Ladies to Cross the Road, Unless You're an Old Lady, in Which Case You Should Watch Good. Like that. Then I changed my mind and did a rewrite. I got it down to about eight hundred commandments. But even that was a little cumbersome. So I rewrote again and got it down to a hundred. Then all the way down to fifteen. Only Moses told me, 'They'll never sit still for fifteen commandments, make it eight.' And I said twelve. And he said nine. And I said ten. And he said *sold*. But he was wrong anyway. They don't even sit still for ten."

22

"Well, you may think we've disappointed you, but you've disappointed us." Imagine me coming on to Him that way, but somehow I found the nerve and I had to say it. "How can you permit the suffering that goes on in the world?"

"I don't. You do," He said.

"You're not involved."

"Listen—I keep up. I know what's going on. Of course, I don't read enough. I mean nonfiction I never read because, after all, I know everything. Fiction I could read more of. But mostly I prefer television."

"You watch television?"

"The news I don't watch because nothing on the news is news to me. Flip Wilson I like. He puts on a zippy show. Sports I watch. Except baseball I don't like too much on television. It's better in the ball park."

"I'm having a lot of trouble focusing on what it is you do."

"That's just it. Most of what I do, I did. I created the world, which is something. In six days. I work very fast. But now I just sort of watch over it. I guess you can say in a sense I'm retired."

"Right. Exactly what a lot of people feel today. God is retired, absent, dead. The same thing."

"It's not. Retired means I'm around, only I'm not as active. Look at it this way. In the old days, I had a lot more to do, setting things up. That's why I put in so many more appearances back then. Now I sit, I watch, I take a walk."

"You take a walk?"

"In the metaphysical sense. Don't try to understand it. But I see everything. I listen to everything. Even the new music. I can't get no-o satis-fac-tion. Also while I'm on this topic, there was one popular song a while back about believing that for every drop of rain that falls, a flower grows. Well, I want to straighten that out while I'm here. There is some rain that just falls. It just falls. It has nothing to do with flowers."

I was in way over my head—was I ever!—but I was trying to organize in my mind what He was saying.

"Well, it seems to me, if you're not as active as you once were, maybe that's why people are losing faith."

"So that's why I'm here. I'm a little worried. People today, they'll worship, who knows what? Like I used to think maybe they'd end up worshiping a car. God would be the 1940 Lincoln Continental. Now I sometimes think it could be an experience, like flying first-class to Hawaii, eating a steak and watching a movie. That could be a God-thing."

"Yes, but looking at it from our standpoint, frankly, how much more are you offering?"

"Listen to him. I got myself a real ipsy-pipsy here."

"What I mean is—God finally reveals Himself in our time and what is His message? I'm not too active, so why don't you stumble along? I hope you make it."

"Such a smart fella and you missed the point. Now write this down, word for word, so nobody else should miss it. The thing is—to use the expression—God lives!

24

This is important. If God was dead or never was, *then* you should be plenty worried because you wouldn't know if what you got can even work. But God is here and He's giving you a guarantee. I'm telling you that I set all this up for you and made it so it *can* work. Only the deal is *you* have to work at it and you shouldn't look to me to do it for you. So? That's not hopeful?"

"Possibly."

"Possibly he gives me. Go. Tell them what I said. God says they got everything they need—it's all built in, and on that I give my word."

I wrote it down word for word.

"And make sure the story gets placed good, so lots of people will read it," He said.

It was apparent the interview was over. I didn't know what was appropriate to say. Do you say "Amen?" I said, "Thank you."

"That's all right. I'll tell you what. You been such a good fella, I'll give you a little personal advice. Your last play. It's not bad, but you got third act trouble. If you cut a little from Act II and combine it with Act III and make it a two act play, you'll have something good. Listen to me. I know from this."

3

I LEFT the room in a numbed condition, took the elevator down and a taxi home, checking my notebook constantly to reassure myself that I had it. Yes, there it was,
the Word of God just as He spoke it, in my own handwriting.

An irrelevant comment about my handwriting. Nobody but me can make it out and sometimes I can't even
make it out. At some point in my life, I stopped trusting

my ability to read back my own handwriting and started relying on memory to make out my notes. So by the time I got home I was very anxious about getting it all transcribed with my typewriter.

When Judy came home, I was rather pretentious.

"Honey, I can't talk to you just now. I've got work. I interviewed God today."

"Is that a new rock group?"

You have to understand, Judy worked for a record company, so that was her orientation.

"No. God! *Him.*"

"*The* Him?"

"Yes. The Divine Power. Saying the words overwhelmed me with my own importance. Emitting beatification, I elegantly returned to the typing of my notes.

When I was finished, Judy was waiting for me.

"God, you said?"

I showed her the letter, showed her the transcript and reported that I, of all men on earth, had been chosen to receive The Word of God.

"Did you make this up?"

"No, Honey, I'm telling you. I was chosen."

She read the transcript carefully.

"Sort of a colloquial God, isn't He?"

"He's talking like that for me."

"Well, I think it's good satire, but I don't think anybody will publish it."

"It is not satire. It is fact. Truth. Divine Truth!"

Now my wife knows me pretty well and she knows when I'm kidding. Something about the zealot's look in my eyes told her I wasn't kidding.

"My poor darling," she said.

"What poor darling? I have heard God. He spoke to me. I have been chosen."

The next few moments are subject to dispute. Judy claims I went transfixed for about ten minutes. I claim it was just, as I say, the next few moments. But the enormity of it all was beginning to get through to me.

Somewhere I dimly heard Judy saying:

"You know, I really do believe you believe this. Which I suppose on some level is the same as it really happening to you."

"It happened. It happened to me."

"Yes, darling, and we do have some signs—the fact that you chose to be a playwright, your need to create fantasy lives in your work, your recent feelings of rejection in this area, compounding a need to exalt yourself." My wife was in analysis.

Judy then made an emergency phonecall to her doctor, outlining my predicament and asking her to come over. She wouldn't. Her analyst doesn't make housecalls. She did make a couple of suggestions, though. First, that I definitely come in to see her the following morning. Second, failing that—we make the most of it and try to sell it to *Playboy*.

"It is not fiction," I said. "I know the difference between fiction and nonfiction."

"Don't you mean fantasy and reality?"

"I know that, too."

"Honey, how can this be? You're not a religious person. You don't even go to a synagogue."

"That wasn't a requirement. He's God over everybody. He could have talked to anybody."

"Yes, that's what I'm trying to reason out with you. Why would He have chosen to talk to *you?*"

"He knows my work."

She took my hands and spoke to me the way you'd reason with a child.

"You're a wonderful person and a wonderful writer, but think about it—out of all the people in the world . . ."

"We should just accept it for the miracle it is," I said, becoming saintly again.

"I can't accept it."

At this point, my answer to my wife, drawn from the depths of my theological knowledge—my three shaky years of Hebrew School and all those *Bible Comics*—was successful in moving her to a position of partial doubt.

"If you believe in God at all, you could believe He appeared to Man in biblical times. If He appeared in the past, He could appear in the present. If He appeared in the past to ordinary men, which, if you remember your Bible, He did—then He could appear in the present to an ordinary man. If He could appear to an ordinary man, He could appear to me. So if you be-

29

lieve in God, you could believe He could appear to me."

"I'm not so sure," she said.

"Thank you," I replied, ready to settle for anything.

"And I think tomorrow morning you should see my doctor."

"I will not go to your shrink!" I shouted. "I have just had the most important experience of my life, of any man's life, and as my wife you have a responsibility to stand by me. Do you think I could make all this up? Why would I? Believe! That is the key word. That is why God came to us, through me, using me as a vessel for His thoughts. Oh, I don't claim any particular uniqueness or majesty. Just that of an ordinary man, chosen by God to deliver His message. God lives! It is so. And I will go forth and deliver His message."

It was all pretty high-blown, but I was caught up in my newly acquired religious fervor.

"I still think you should see a doctor," Judy said rather quietly. But as I glared at her with my new Billy Graham eyes, she added, "Or else I think you should sell it to *Playboy*."

Playboy was certainly out of the question. It just wouldn't do to have The Word of God in there with all those breasts. Later on somebody from *Playboy* did contact me and said why hadn't I thought of them? They could have run it in the front of the book as a *Playboy* Interview because, after all, didn't they do Bertrand Russell once and wouldn't I think of them the next time something comes up, such as Moses?

30

I decided to take it to *Life* magazine. *Life* had a big circulation and paid pretty well, too, but that really wasn't a consideration, since I wasn't sure I was going to keep the money. Already I was getting purer for the experience.

I went to see my friend Harry, an editor at *Life*, who listened to my story, which by now included a very strong statement about how this was the real thing and not satire. He read the transcript, then made a phonecall. It wasn't to another editor, it was to my wife.

"He says he's seen God, Judy."

"Not seen—*heard*," I said.

"He needs help, Judy."

"Not help. A cover story. Or maybe a special issue, but at least a cover story," I said.

Judy told him she knew all about it, that she felt I was absolutely serious and she was planning to discuss it with her doctor at her next session. My friend turned back to me, looking worried. Frightened, I think is the word.

"You say this really happened?"

"Believe. It's true."

"Quit putting me on. You're kidding, right?"

"It's the Wonder of Wonders, the Miracle of Miracles."

"The Miracle of Miracles, huh?"

He was looking around the office, checking out his escape routes. Wherein I re-emphasized my sanity and launched into my moving speech about believing.

"I think the way to handle this is to say, I pass."

"That's sacrilege! You can't."

"All right. Let's be logical, as if that would do any good. You claim you interviewed God. Where's your proof?"

"God says He doesn't do proof."

"But I'm not talking to God. Where's *your* proof?"

"Harry, don't you understand? The message is the message. God says, 'Believe.' If you believe, there's your proof."

"Have you got tapes?"

"No tapes."

"How about pictures?"

"What's the matter with you? This is God. No pictures."

"Why?"

"It's like ghosts."

"Look, I don't think I'm qualified to deal with you . . ."

"I'm not nuts. You're nuts! This is the biggest story ever."

"Even if I believed you, I wouldn't believe you. But certainly not without proof. Tapes and pictures. Fingerprints if you've got them. No, I don't mean that."

"Aha! A little frightened, aren't you? Because maybe it *is* true. And maybe you just offended Him with that dumb little remark."

"That's ridiculous."

"Is it? Suppose I tell you He's listening right now."

"It's beyond reason."

"A typical lack of faith."

"Take it to the *Reader's Digest*. They love God. Better yet, go on a long vacation and rest your head."

"I'll take it to another editor. You're not the final word around here. I won't have God penalized for your religious hangups," I said, picking up my material. "You deserve His wrath on you for this. You're just lucky He doesn't get into this kind of stuff."

"I know. I read your piece."

"Goddamn you!" I said, pausing for the full effect. "He heard that, you know."

At home I wrote a letter to the managing editor of *Life:*

It is a measure of the lack of faith in the times in which we live, that if a man has spoken with God, he must protect himself from ridicule. He will not be believed. It is beyond reason, simply incredible, the doubters will say. But I have spoken with God. Not because of any specialness on my part, but out of God's desire at this time in man's existence to communicate through an ordinary man, who can in turn communicate with other ordinary men. The transcript of our conversation is available to *Life* magazine, and through *Life*, to the world.

I am an established writer of good standing, and mention this to offset any doubts you may have as to credibility. As to the believability of the miracle itself, the transcript and facts speak for themselves. I will follow up with a phonecall to your office, to arrange for the turning over to you—without payment—of this, the most important news story in the history of the world.

Thinking back over that note, I realize there was nothing in it to convince them I was anything but a crackpot. But you get caught up in it.

I decided to give it more weight by sending it as a telegram, along with copies to several of *Life*'s senior editors. I followed up the telegrams with a series of phonecalls, but everybody was out to me. So I sent another telegram informing them that a messenger would hand-deliver the transcript to their offices the next day.

Dressed as a messenger, I personally hand-delivered the transcript.

Just one day later, which is pretty fast response in that business, I received the transcript back by return mail along with a note from them:

We regret that we are unable to use the enclosed material. Our present supply of manuscripts of this type is adequate for our current needs. We wish you success in sending your manuscript elsewhere.

Life magazine had rejected God.

4

THE NEXT thing I did was to send the same telegram to several editors at *The New York Times.* I got an almost immediate phonecall from a *Times* reporter who said he was following it up. I thought that was a terrific beginning and I had visions of a front-page story with an eight-column headline right across the page. Only it turned out he was putting together a wrap-up story for a possible Sunday feature on "Recent Divine Revelations," combining me with a 14-year-old Brooklyn schoolgirl who claimed to have seen the Virgin Mary, the third Virgin Mary sighting in recent months, and an 83-year-old lady in Queens who claimed to have spoken with Joan of Arc.

I wasn't going to diddle around any longer. I decided to break the news of the interview on a big scale. I prepared a press release for news editors of all the major newspapers, magazines and radio and television stations, calling for a press conference. I suppose coming right at the news head on sounded just as eccentric as my telegram, but at this stage I really thought the best way to do it was state the facts just as they were.

> *For immediate release:*
>
> MAJOR MIRACLE: GOD HAS SPOKEN IN OUR TIME
>
> The Divine Power's voice was heard in New York this week in the first miracle of its kind in modern times.
>
> In a far-ranging discussion with a 36-year-old American writer, the Supreme Being criticized skeptics who have said God is dead or irrelevant. He reaffirmed His Divine Presence and the viability of civilization—cautioning, however, that Man should not look to God to make it work.

The press release then went on to fill in details of the meeting with God, some background facts on me and then called for the press conference at noon, two days later at Manhattan Center, where I rented a ballroom.

Manhattan Center is a large building on Thirty-

36

fourth Street in Manhattan where unions hold their meetings, public schools graduate, Polish and Latin bands play Saturday night dances—and now God's word would be passed on to the world.

Just a few members of the press showed up. Judy was there and there was a *Newsweek* reporter, a camera crew from ABC-TV News, someone from WINS Radio, a New York *News* photographer, and a hippy from an underground ecology newspaper called *The Good Earth*. Well, it was a start.

I began with a short opening statement.

"First of all, this is true. It really happened. God spoke to me." I looked at my audience. There was no reaction. I then told them about receiving the letter and about going to the room on Madison Avenue. No reaction. Then I described the interview itself. No reaction. They were just sitting, expressionless. Then I went into my little speech on why they should believe. Still no reaction. So I decided to ask for questions.

"All right, what's the gimmick?" said the WINS man.

"There is no gimmick. It is simply a miracle."

"You're not plugging something?"

"I am not plugging anything. I am a conduit for The Word of God."

"This isn't for a book or a movie or something?"

"It is not."

"Crap!" he said. Crap! And he started packing up to leave. And so did the others. I couldn't believe it.

"Wait. Where are you going?" I stepped in front of

the *Newsweek* guy and blocked his path. "What is this?"

He patted me on the shoulder condescendingly and said, "Sorry. There's no story in it for us."

"No story?"

"I saw your piece on The Stones. I thought something might be cooking."

"This is God! He's bigger than The Stones!"

"Free-lancing stinks," he said. "You need a vacation."

"You've got to believe me!"

"Look fella, I'm doing a piece on press agentry. That's why I came. But this . . ."

He patted me on the shoulder again, in a gesture that was all pity and he walked away. I turned to the camera crew.

"What about you guys?"

"For this we can shoot the guy on Broadway with the Bibles."

They were all leaving!

"Don't you have any questions? Don't you want to make sure?" They were sure. "Don't you even want to see the transcript?" They didn't want to see the transcript.

Can you imagine the nerve of those people? They all came because when they saw it was about God, they thought it might be some kind of publicity stunt—and they were disappointed because it only turned out to be the real thing.

The hippy from *The Good Earth* remained. He was

38

about twenty-two, wearing dungarees, a western shirt and sandals. He sat relaxed with his feet up on a chair.

"The establishment press for you," he said.

"They just walked out on God," I said, desolate.

"God. That's beautiful, man. You can't beat that."

Judy threw him a look that said—what are you doing? Don't encourage him. But I didn't need much encouragement.

"And you believe it?"

"I'll put it this way. I may not believe it. But then I don't not believe it."

"I'll buy that," I said.

"There's been a few people I know say they saw God. Mostly on acid."

"This wasn't on acid. It just was."

"Beautiful."

"Would you like to see the transcript?"

"Sure."

He read it slowly, nodding his head every few sentences. Finally, he looked up at me.

"Heavy, man."

"And you believe it?"

"Like I say. I don't not. But then it's not for me to judge."

He was still with me. I'd been turned down by *Life*, the *Times*, *Newsweek*, ABC-TV, WINS, the *News*, but he was still with me. Judy knew what I was thinking and jumped in.

"Honey, isn't it clear that people just can't accept

39

this. All those reporters who left. All the reporters who didn't even show. It's time to forget it."

"But there's interest. We have here a fellow with a publication. By the way, could I see it?"

He produced a copy of *The Good Earth,* a twelve-page newspaper, rather shabbily printed, militantly anti-establishment, and all within ecological terms. There were articles like "The Major Murderers" listing names of polluting corporations. A section called "The Murdered" with pictures of human corpses, dead fish and birds. The main body of the paper was six pages called "Dire Warnings" listing a series of pessimistic speculations about the end of the world. Its heart was in the right place, though, and what if it were a publication of zealots—I had become a zealot myself.

"This is perfect. What better place to run an interview with God than in a publication devoted to man's continuance? It's yours. Exclusive."

"You know we only run stuff the establishment press won't touch."

"You just saw."

"That's true."

He looked at the transcript again.

"God?"

"God!"

"It's possible, I guess."

"It's a miracle."

"Well, why don't we let the public decide?"

"Why don't we?"

Judy was dying.

"We'll run it."

"You got it."

We shook hands on it.

"By the way, what's your circulation?"

"One hundred thousand."

"One hundred thousand? That many?"

"Don't underestimate the underground, man."

I wouldn't—ever again. That one issue of *The Good Earth* would start the chain that would turn the world upside down, especially me.

5

The Good Earth was put out by three former editors of college newspapers. I had met Jimmy, the editor in chief. The others were a fairly square-looking boy named Ralph and Rita, a gorgeous girl who was completely unconcerned with her own gorgeousness. They were all gorgeous, really. They got very excited about the interview and I don't want to go into a whole thing about kids often being more sensitive to important issues than their elders, but without them, it wouldn't have happened.

The story was laid out with a big headline, "An Interview with God," and we worked on an opening paragraph to set the stage for the interview itself. It told who I was and that the following was presented not as fiction or satire, but as an actual interview that I said I had experienced. Then came the interview, complete. And then some observations by me on the basic need to believe and the simple logic of it—"If He appeared in the past to ordinary men . . ." Then a statement by the editors declaring that as far as they could determine, this was a non-drug experience, that they weren't judging its verity, not having been there . . . and finally, that they were running it because the establishment press had no balls.

It all ran to four pages and they decided it was so important they would kill everything else and just put it out as a four-page paper. And there it was. Thanks to these kids, I had my special issue.

The first thing I learned about the underground press is that it's not so underground. I had this image of publications smuggled inside of suitcases. But a lot of underground newspapers are sold over the counter at newsstands and on college campuses and through mail subscriptions. You could get *The Good Earth* on the west coast, at hipper colleges around the country and at several locations in New York City, alongside the other

43

offbeat papers, which were mostly sex exploitation jobs. It was bought largely by kids, but occasionally by a pervert busy buying up every sex newspaper at a newsstand and thinking that *The Good Earth* was a euphemism for Good Sex or something.

I was very pleased with the way the issue finally looked. The kids at the paper assured me it would go over well, only it might take a while to happen. It would be a couple of weeks before the paper got to the west coast, even longer for it to get filtered through to some of the midwest colleges, and they were always behind in the office on subscription mailings. So there was no way at the moment of judging its full impact. Meantime, I drifted around the city checking on newsstand sales, waiting for the public reaction and covering myself by personally mailing copies of the issue to all the members of the press I felt were important. A little public relations idea. I'm not married to a publicist for nothing.

That particular lady was going through a very bad time. She didn't know if she was married to a maniac or a drifter. What was upsetting her was the fact that I refused to admit my temporary insanity. Notice "temporary" insanity. Judy, out of love, I presume, was not prepared to say I was permanently insane. But I refused to see her doctor. I refused to say the interview was a figment of my temporarily confused mind. And worst of all for an executive wife married to a free-lancer, I refused to work on anything else to make money while

44

awaiting the snowballing effect to my interview. This accounts for me being labeled a drifter as well as a maniac.

I waited and for the first few weeks, nothing happened. The kids said it was too early, the copies were still filtering through. But there were no letters coming into the paper. There was no response from the regular press to the issues I sent out. I was impatient. Judy was unhappy. And it turns out, so was He. One day I opened my mail to find:

```
What's with this Good Earth? Life maybe.
Time! Newsweek! But The Good Earth? You
better come and talk. Same place, Wednesday
at 6 p.m.
```

In the long sweep of history, there have been a lot of men called up on the carpet, but this was the ultimate. Warily, I went to 600 Madison Avenue, pressed the elevator for 26 and got out at 37 again. The intercom was in the room waiting for me. Out of it came His voice.

"*Nu?*" He said.

"Hello, God," I said, trying not to look nervous.

"So? *The Good Earth?* You call that coverage?"

"One hundred thousand circulation!"

"Peanuts. I'm God over billions. He delivers one hundred thousand."

"But nobody else wanted the story."

The next thing He said was kind of cruel.

"I think I bet on a *pisher.*"

45

"I'm not that," I said, oozing guilt and remorse.

"I give a fella a story, a hot story, exclusive yet. He buries it. You got your *Time,* your *Newsweek,* your Walter Cronkite . . ."

"But they turned it down."

"For this I showed up? I'm God. I don't have to do this."

"It's not so bad. It was a special issue. I thought it looked pretty good."

"They're nice kids, but they got no readership."

"I tried."

"You tried."

"I did. Did you see? *Life,* the *Times,* the press conference . . ."

"Okay. You tried. I take it back. You're not a *pisher.* But you're not a Hearst either. Hearst! What he would have done with this."

But I had tried and I had cared and I didn't know why He was blaming me.

"You know, maybe if you show up and nobody is very knocked out about the story, that's not a reason to blame the reporter. Maybe it has more to do with your basic relationship to Man."

There was no answer. Then He said, "You might have a point. All right, forget it. I don't blame you."

I felt the fires of purgatory diminishing.

"But an underground newspaper! Page One all over it should have been. I could have seen to it. But I don't get into managing the news."

"They said it would take a while. We still don't know the full result."

"So I'll wait a little longer. I got nothing better to do. But I'll tell you this—if it doesn't make more of a to-do than up to now—you'll think of something, okay?"

"Okay."

Who was I kidding? What could I do? The discussion having been left on that open-ended note, I went home, half hoping to blot it all out with a nice coma. Lacking the ability to do that, I did the next best thing. I developed a beautiful psychological cold, requiring my wife to attend me constantly with hot tea, aspirin and vitamin C, thereby restoring the balance of our relationship from maniac-accuser versus maniac, to wife and unwell husband. I managed to milk the situation for three days, remaining in bed the whole time watching television. On a Friday night, I had the news on. David Brinkley, who often concludes his segment on NBC with a wry remark, had this to say:

"And finally this note. An underground newspaper of ecology which calls itself *The Good Earth* has printed an exclusive interview in a special edition. This would not normally command the attention of a network news program, but the interview claims to be with God. Yes —God. And on the outside chance that it could be true, this reporter would like to hedge his bets. So if He's listening, let God know, we *did* report it. We did not scoff. Thank you and goodnight for NBC News."

It was a brand-new ball game.

6

WHAT HAPPENED next, to clean up the expression for the clergy reading this, is that the snowball hit the fan. After that newscast, NBC and *The Good Earth* were deluged with inquiries. People were curious—the press, the public, believers, agnostics, kids on campuses, old ladies in the Bible Belt. The printer pleaded with the staff to go back to press and they ran off another 25,000 copies which were gobbled up within a week. The printer himself put up the money for a rush job of 50,000 more and even that didn't seem enough.

It became one of those delicious get-even moments of life. The media, from whom I couldn't buy a base hit, were now scrambling all over each other to get to me. There were reporters at the door and phonecalls day and night. It got so that I had to hire somebody just to deal with the press, and in one of the most obviously nepotistic moves ever, I hired Judy.

I should interject that Judy had been considering quitting her job for some time and this was a good excuse. But I don't know why—and forgive me for airing this in public, Dear—is Women's Lib and the traditional exploitation of women sufficient reason that I had to pay her a salary out of my own pocket?

Still, she was a real ace; schooled in the booking of rock music groups on rounds of press interviews, she started booking me as though I were a rock group. We worked out a stock interview containing the basic details of my encounter with God, and for the next couple of weeks, this is what I passed on to the press—over breakfast, over lunch, over dinner, over tea and cheesecake, over late-night corned beef sandwiches. A small personal note. During this period, I gained several pounds and got hives.

Mostly the reporters wanted to determine if I was a nut. Since I was not, and since I had my efficient and stable wife present to dignify the interviews and me, they had no easy out. The path most of them chose was not to comment on the factuality of the interview with God—nobody was committing himself on that, but to report what they considered to be the hard news of the story, that an underground newspaper called *The Good Earth* had run the interview, that the interviewer claimed it to be true and that the issue was in great demand.

There's a funny kind of escalation the media get into here. They help create a news event in the first place—in this case by mentioning a newspaper—and in so doing, create a demand for it. Then they report the demand, which is essentially reporting on the results of their reporting. But who was I to argue? It wasn't a Page-One story yet, but it was getting picked up. The fact that so many copies of the paper were cleaned out in a short time was something the press could use, and it was reported over the wire services, in the major city newspapers, on the network news shows and in *Time* and *Newsweek* in their Press columns. I was delighted, which was naïve of me, because what hit the fan next wasn't a snowball, it was metaphysical backlash.

On the next weekend I was vilified in over 200 church sermons, and to show how ecumenical the anger was, in 30 Saturday synagogue sermons. Typical of the comments were those of a Baptist minister in Sumter, South Carolina, J. B. Kearnsworth, who said, "This charlatan, this snake in the garden of God's creatures . . ."—meaning me—"This vileness who would

50

so defame the name of our Lord and seek to raise himself from his degraded state, this lowly liar and clown . . ." Well, I had clearly offended many men of the cloth, in my opinion because I had upset the traditional lines of communication between themselves, their flocks and God, and this undercut their sense of power and I don't care if I get in trouble with them for saying it, since I got in enough trouble anyway.

They railed on. A pastor in Alabama called me a menace. And a rabbi in Brooklyn called me a *shmuck*.

Their diatribes even extended to the kids on the newspaper and that really bothered me, but the kids laughed it off. They were having a terrific time living with the sudden success of their paper and were all excited about taking advantage of their new-found audience with their next big "Murderers of the Environment" issue—and did I want to pitch in? I could have "Deaths from Asphyxiation."

I was preoccupied with the backlash. There were some telegrams to the White House calling for my deportation. To where? I came from here. A few newsstands had their copies of *The Good Earth* "confiscated" by vigilante groups, and there was one organized letter-writing campaign to the press protesting the publicity given the interview, all using the phrase "conspiratorial-communist-eastern-faggot-establishment press." But these were largely restricted to pockets of anger around the country. The big city religious leaders and the tonier organizations such as the Roman Catholic Archdiocese in New York and Temple Emanu-El chose to ignore the interview completely.

The media dutifully reported the volume of mail they had been receiving in response to their own reporting of their own story, which is more escalating your own escalation and that became the new wrinkle on the old news.

Then came the next big news break. On a Saturday night in a nationwide telecast from the Astrodome in Houston, Texas, I made Billy Graham.

Now if you're Billy Graham and somebody is going around saying he interviewed God, and it is reported widely in the press, and there are thousands of copies of the interview in circulation, with hundreds of clergymen devoting their sermons to the subject, at some point you're going to have to say something.

But if you're Billy Graham, you're also intelligent and sophisticated in the ways of media and religious controversy and you're not going to become embroiled in a Holy War. So what he did was take the safe middle of the road. I say middle of the road, because at one extreme he could have vilified me or, on the other hand, just believed me. What he chose to do was simply acknowledge me. He mentioned the interview and declared that "his insistence on its validity was simply one more example of Man's deep need to know God." Billy Graham. He had gotten himself off the hook.

It was important, though. Having Billy Graham mention your conversation with God, no matter how equivocally, is still great publicity. Judy was elated. Somewhere along the line, maybe out of self-protection, or maybe just out of concern for our relationship, she managed a subtle bit of repression on herself. As we got more involved in dealing with the press, she began to completely ignore the original reason for the publicity —the actual interview with God. She started to focus instead on the *mechanics* of the publicity, worrying about the quality of interviews, the quantity of pickups in the press, the number of people reached. In fact, it was taking her over. She was all caught up in the project, plunging on as though she were pushing a hit rock recording. Now if your wife begins to block out areas, which if you discussed, would get you in trouble, and decides instead to fixate on something else which you need anyway, you go along with it.

"Yes, Honey, Billy Graham. That's terrific," I said.

"It's more than terrific. It gives you legitimacy."

"I thought I had that before."

"You didn't. But how can you understand, Darling? You're a non-professional."

Yes, she was really caught up in it. Professional that she was, she announced to me, *her* zealot's eyes flashing, that it was time to call another press conference.

Moving up in class, we scheduled it for the Overseas Press Club in New York. Judy prepared a special press kit for the occasion, a glossy cardboard folder containing the issue of *The Good Earth,* reprints of subsequent news stories in the press, a biographical data sheet on me, and an overall news release for the press conference, which Judy had dubbed, "An Affirmation"—words which appeared in gothic letters on the cover of the kit.

I watched the hall filling up—lights and microphones were being set up, photographers were crouching around, newsmen I'd seen on television and who were themselves celebrities to me, were taking their places—and I was beginning to get very nervous.

"Did we really need that press kit? Isn't it too flashy?"

"It's perfect," Judy said.

"But it looks like we're overselling. Couldn't I have just made a simple statement?"

"That's not the way it works. They need material to work with."

"How much did all that cost me anyway?"

"Nine hundred sixty dollars."

"Nine hundred sixty dollars?"

"You'll more than get it back."

"From God?"

"In results."

Nine hundred sixty dollars. I hoped God appreciated what I was doing for Him.

We were ready to start and it was mobbed. I introduced myself and explained that I would make a brief statement and then entertain questions from the floor.

"Members of the press, if you find this hard to believe, well, so do I. But it did happen. I did interview God. And my only objective here is to affirm this fact. I have no other motive, profit or otherwise. To prove that, I have just learned that your press kits are costing me out of my own pocket to the tune of nine hundred sixty dollars"—at which point I laughed nervously and too loudly. There was dead silence. A hall full of people staring at me.

"Well, it's called 'An Affirmation' and that is what I would like to do. I affirm that I spoke with God. I affirm that the interview as printed in this newspaper is an accurate report of the discussion. And I further affirm that I spoke with God again since then and He was somewhat unhappy with the treatment the interview was originally given."

There was an immediate stir in the room. This was something new. They knew about the first conversation, or as the press liked to describe it, the *alleged* first conversation. Now there was an alleged second one, and the pencils and flashbulbs were flying.

"Finally, I would like to say there is another affirmation, not mine, yours, and that of all men. The affirmation of faith in God you must make in order to believe what I have told you to be true."

I think that last part was a nice way to end. But there's no such thing as weaving a mood in a room full of hungry reporters. Twenty people started shouting at once. I thought each reporter would announce himself neatly, like "So and so of the *Washington Post*. My question is . . ." The questions came shooting up at me from all sides, reporters all over each other's lines.

"What did God say to you the second time?" someone shouted.

"He reprimanded me. It seems He had hoped for a bigger coverage of the story."

"He said that to you?"

"But I told Him *you* people made those decisions." A little gamesmanship.

"Where and how did this second conversation take place?"

"The same circumstances as the first."

"What else was said?"

"We talked mostly circulation figures."

"Circulation figures?"

"He knows a lot about it. He knows a lot about everything, if you think about it."

"And He was unhappy with the *coverage*, you say? He used that word?"

"Yes. He agreed to wait and see if a bigger story develops. But I guess that's up to you."

"Now one minute!" An angry looking man jumped up. "Are you threatening us?"

"No, I'm just telling what happened."

"And what if we think this is a prank?"

Out of conviction, which I had, and also out of a sense of the need for a public performance, which I knew was required, I drew myself up and in my most offended and earnest manner, I said:

"This is no prank. And I am not keeping you here, sir,

56

if you feel you are wasting your time. But I tell you that this is the truth!"

There was applause and someone yelled, "Right on!" It was coming from my kids, Jimmy, Ralph and Rita, but in what had to be a small turning point, there was also a scattering of applause from other people, from strangers.

"What would a naturally skeptical man find in your story to make him believe it?"

"Only my word and His."

"What documentation do you have?"

The questions were coming from every part of the room.

"Only my word and His."

"Would you consent to a psychological test for stability?"

"I think that submitting to a test of the validity of God's word, is probably by extension, profane, but I would do so."

I could just see the headlines: "GOD REPORTER" OKAYS LOONEY TEST.

"Assuming this is true, just assuming, do you think you're qualified for the position you're in?"

"No I don't. I would have preferred someone else, especially at this moment."

That got a little laugh. It's hard to resist being a performer up there, but I tried to catch myself.

"However, I think I'm just as capable as the next person in wondering about God, and to quote Billy Graham —a little deft name dropping there—mine 'is just one more example of Man's deep need to know God.' "

On this note, a little lady who had been sitting quietly in the back screamed, "Hallelujah! Praise Be The Lord!"

It scared me and everyone else. Then she did it again. "Hallelujah! Praise Be The Lord!"

A guard came to remove her, but the little lady wouldn't budge and rather than make a larger scene, we went on.

"Do you think God will reveal Himself to you again as you claim He has?"

"I don't speak for Him. Let me stress that. I'm just passing on what God said to me."

Suddenly a man shouted, "God is Glory! God is Glory!" which keyed off the "Hallelujah! Praise Be The Lord!" lady—and the two of them were shouting in tandem—"God is Glory! God is Glory!" "Hallelujah! Praise Be The Lord!"

I said to myself, Jesus Christ! It's a scene out of *Elmer Gantry!*

The guard quieted them down and we tried to get back to business, which then turned a bit ugly.

Someone rose and pointed his finger at me, shouting, "I submit you are a dangerous man, as the outburst a moment ago will attest. Innocent people can be aroused by your irresponsible behavior."

58

"Is that a question?" A little debating point I learned from watching Presidential news conferences.

"The only question, sir, is your sanity!"

He had his satisfaction and as he sat down he was greeted by some yeas and boos, which combined with a few more "Hallelujah! Praise Be The Lord's" and a "God is Glory! God is Glory!" and the whole damn thing was falling apart.

I hurried to make a closing statement, asking them, if nothing else, as reporters to report my contentions and finally, reaffirmed my affirmation. I rushed through it very fast, like an old Danny Kaye song, because I had just about run out of press conference. Somebody was shouting invectives at me, there were hot arguments on the floor, guards were trying to control the "Hallelu-jahs" and the "God is Glory's" and there were a few "Amens" in there by now. All I could say was "Thank you for coming" which no one heard anyway and with the room in disorder, like bad children, Judy and I fled.

That night there was formed an "Ad Hoc Committee to Protest the Debasement of God," made up of assorted clergymen and private citizens. They held a press conference of their own and denounced me.

What they really accomplished was to give me more publicity. The following day *The New York Times* did a combined report of my press conference and their press conference—with pictures!

It had taken a while, but God was finally Page One.

7

THE CONTROVERSY, it was now a controversy, started to pick up momentum. Divinity students were convening in retreats to discuss it—and there were several God-ins on college campuses. The Pope wasn't saying. Eric Sevareid said, but his discourse was so philosophical, I didn't know where he stood. William F. Buckley called me some names I never did understand. Richard Nixon had no comment. Spiro Agnew labeled me a "Godless buffoon." And my mother called from Florida.

"Hello, dear, how are you?"

"Fine."

"How's Judy?"

"Fine."

"Is she pregnant?"

"No, mother."

"Everybody down here is a grandmother . . ."

"Yes, mother."

"So what's with your writing? Making any money? You know, you have to make money because you're not going to have a working wife forever because wives do have babies in some families, knock on wood, I should live to see the day."

"Mother, have you read the papers lately?"

"I read."

"Have you read anything about me?"

"I saw. And on the TV. I was very embarrassed."

"Embarrassed?"

"To say such things about God. That's not nice."

"Not nice?"

"For that I sent you to Hebrew School?"

In the media world, they were keeping up the pace. There was a non-committal editorial in *The Sunday New York Times* about "the salutary effect of thinking of God at all in an increasingly technological society." There were pictures of models posing in the sands of The Holy Land in Harper's Bazaar, somehow tied in editorially with the controversy, and I couldn't see how.

Time magazine, which ran an all-type "Is God Dead?" cover a few years back, re-ran the cover with

61

the word "Dead" crossed out and "Retired?" written in. The battery of God Is Dead theologians who had been out of print for a while were hauled back in to comment on my interview and their consensus was—God is dead.

The article quoted a Los Angeles rabbi, reformed, who said this was bigger than the Dead Sea Scrolls, a rather conservative statement, I thought. A professor of comparative religion at Hope College in the Midwest said "The God Controversy," as it was becoming known, was a true test of Man's faith, and it was fortunate that there lived in our midst a person as pure of soul as me with whom God could communicate, said statement sending old pure-soul me into waves of remorse over the dirty things I had done in my life, like sleeping with ladies before I was married.

Offers began coming in which I chose to decline—would I give interviews about such matters as my taste in food? Clothing? Shoes? Would I lend my name to a book? *The Heavenly Cookbook: Divine Recipes for the Religious Holidays.* Would I come to the Pines Hotel in the Catskill Mountains to speak at their Intellectua-thon? Topics: Is Pre-Marital Sex Necessary? Is God Alive? "The Swinging Weekend for Thinking Singles." And the television talk shows began inviting me to appear, but I felt that type of promotion, appearing alongside the latest star plugging his latest movie wouldn't be dignified. There was a temptation, though. I saw myself sitting with Johnny Carson and when asked about my previous activities, slyly segueing into a discussion of my plays and getting a production out of the deal.

I could have used the money, too. I computed that interviewing God had already cost me nearly $2,000 including Judy's salary, which she insisted on, $200 a week.

She was working, I'll say that, servicing reporters with press kits and giving out stock answers for what were the predictable questions. The phone rang constantly, and one evening after a particularly hectic siege of phonecalls, I received a call from the *Kansas City Star*. I was tired and I answered with the usual line. Yes, it happened. Yes, I am a sane, responsible person. Yes, I would like everyone to accept the truth of the interview—and perhaps because I was tired I broke the rhythm to add, "I also feel deep in my heart that we should be grateful to God for reaching out to us in this time of our need."

When I hung up, Judy was looking at me closely.

"That was a very touching thing you just said. You know, you've been awfully consistent in this. I could almost believe you."

Now it's one thing to be a public personality in the eyes of the public. At least there you can close your door at night. But what if you're public in the eyes of *God?* That night, when Judy and I made love, I had the oddest feeling that He was watching. And wouldn't He then, by the very definition of being God, *always* watch? That's a very creepy concept. So let's not go into it any further.

8

I DIMLY remember from my high school Spanish text-book a story that passed for humor. A teacher asks a class, "Is God everywhere?" and the children say, "Yes, God is in the heavens, in the fields and in the houses." One little boy insists God may be everywhere but not in his basement. It turns out God is not in his basement because he has no basement.

We have a basement. And God was in it.

We live in the ground floor apartment of a brownstone in Manhattan. Judy was taking a nap and I was working in my room when I noticed the desk lamp flickering. I went downstairs to check the fuse box. There, coming out of the hot-water heater, was His voice.

"Hey, it's me. God."

You know those comic strips where somebody gets so scared his hair stands on end?

"You're going to give me a heart attack," I said.

"Don't worry," He said, which is better than Blue Cross. "I've got to meet you here. Outside there are too many reporters following you."

"I suppose. But this is very hard to grasp. How do I relate to a hot-water heater?"

"I'll tell you what. Go upstairs and see if your wife is sleeping."

I went back upstairs and saw that Judy was sleeping soundly. Then I came downstairs again. That's when it happened. He was actually standing there. God! In person!

How do you conceive of God? A tall man in a long white beard? A robed, sceptered presence? A flickering substance with the appearance of shape? I'm here to tell you God was a little, Jewish-looking man. He had poor posture. He was nearly bald. And He was wearing a Nehru suit.

"You're God?"

"Better Satan?"

"But you look like a little Jewish man with poor posture."

65

"Like I keep telling you, it's for empathy. Better I should appear as somebody from your background."

"You're God?" I just stared at Him, dazed. I can't be sure of this, but the way I was staring, I think I made Him uncomfortable. He adjusted the buttons of His jacket.

"Your clothes! That suit!"

"I thought it looked peppy."

God had appeared to me! I sat down on a paint can, shaking my head with wonderment.

"This is just too much for me."

"I know. And in your own basement yet. It's some nifty miracle."

"And this is what you look like . . ."

"This is what I look like for *you*. For somebody else I would look different. And I'll tell you something, but don't make any funny remarks. I can also be a lady."

It was God!

"I can be any color, I can do any face or any voice you name. I'm a regular David Frye."

"I have seen God."

"Look, don't get too carried away. I want to have a nice discussion."

He pulled up a paint can for Himself and sat down. I was sitting face to face with God in front of the hot-water heater, hot-stove-league style.

As we got close, I could tell he was wearing cologne —Canoe.

"You're like a person. Even down to the cologne."

66

"I thought as long as I was getting dressed up . . ."

I was staring again. "Can I touch you? Would I feel you?"

"*Oy-oy-oy*. No, you wouldn't feel me, and let's not get into a science-fiction monkey business about it. We got more important things. Like how it's going . . ."

"I think it's going very well now."

"Well, the kids went back to press a few times. That's okay."

"And the big press conference."

"Yeah, the press conference was okay. The yelling at the end I could have lived without."

"And we made Page One of the *Times*."

"That I would expect."

"And *Time*. A cover story in *Time*."

"I saw. So what about *Newsweek?*"

"Huh?"

"*U.S. News. McCall's*. You going to stop with *Time?* It should be the cover of every magazine, everywhere you look. Like with Ali McGraw when she was hot."

"But I thought—"

"What? God would make conversation with a person and you shouldn't see it everywhere you look? God, who made the heavens and the earth and the doggies and the fishes?"

"Interest is growing."

"And how come no Johnny Carson?"

"That was my decision. I think I should maintain a certain dignity in this."

67

"Dignity? Listen to ipsy-pipsy him. Readership, listenership is what counts."

"I just figured in the long run . . ."

"You could go on Flip Wilson."

"Flip Wilson? It's a variety show!"

"So? You could stand up in the audience and wave."

Some people have William Morris advising them in their careers, not me.

"If you think so."

"I'm not telling you what to do. It's just a suggestion."

Guess who was going to do Flip Wilson?

"But plenty people haven't heard."

I thought to myself, you're pretty hard to please. Maybe *you* should go on television. He knew what I was thinking.

"Of course, I could make appearances myself, but we'd only have people dropping dead from hysterics. No, you're my fella for better or worse and it's not bad, but it could be better."

"I'll try my best."

"That's all I ask."

"Yes, Sir."

"Sir? What am I, a British knight? You can just call me God."

"Yes, God." Yes, God?

"So listen. Goodbye for now. It's been good seeing you."

How do you reply? It's been incredible *seeing you?* I was speechless. He waved goodbye and waited for me

68

to leave. I went up the stairs, turned to look back, but He was gone.

Judy was stirring from her nap.

"Did I hear you talking to someone?"

"God."

"Here?"

"In the basement."

"You say His voice was in the basement?"

"Not just His voice. Him."

"You're saying you saw Him?"

"I saw God."

"Downstairs?"

"By the hot-water heater."

She started for the basement stairs.

"What did He look like?"

"Like somebody's Jewish uncle."

Judy went down the steps with me following.

"Well, He doesn't seem to be here now, does He?"

"Nope."

"What's that smell—perfume?"

"Cologne."

"Cologne?" she said, sniffing me.

"No, it's not from me. It's God's. You see, He was wearing Canoe."

9

How is it if God was only creating the illusion of appearance for me, that Judy was able to smell the cologne also? A little mystery plot here. And why, the detective asks, should I have smelled anything at all? I did mention this later on and it seemed so insignificant to Him, all He bothered to say was:

"Don't hock me with that. It happens to have a strong scent."

I bring this up only to illustrate that if I had questions, imagine what other people were going through. Theologians, for example. I don't mean the power-minded ones who were busy calling me names. I mean responsible, sensitive theologians, sincerely concerned with Man's relationship to God.

There was a group of such scholars who came together from time to time at Georgetown University to discuss contemporary matters in theology, and nothing could be more important to them than the possibility of somebody having conversations with God. They called a special meeting of their group, which consisted of a Jesuit professor from Georgetown, an expert in eastern religions from Columbia, and professors from Yeshiva University, Brigham Young, Southern Methodist University and Princeton, all PhDs and a very prestigious assemblage.

I was invited to appear before them. I thought, considering their credentials, that just meeting them would be valuable publicity, so I arranged to fly down to Washington—and at their expense. A car and driver met me at the airport and took me to my suite at The Georgetown Inn. I must say the celebrityness of it felt pretty good. I went on to the University for the first meeting, which was held around a long table in an impressive library.

They were very direct. What they wanted to do was establish for themselves an accurate picture of what I claimed to have happened. They were going to ask me a great many questions, some that might seem to me tan-

71

gential, but which they felt would have a bearing on the credibility of my story. So they asked me about the interview, but they also got into areas I was unprepared for, questions about my background and things that never come up in ordinary conversation—like moral questions, philosophical questions, Bar Mitzvah-type questions:

"Did you feel close to God at your Bar Mitzvah?"

"Do you remember your Haftorah?"

"Can you sing it?" I couldn't.

"What does it mean?" I didn't know what it meant *then.*

"What is your personal philosophy?" How do you answer a question like that? I never even thought about it—my personal philosophy.

"I don't know. Do unto others . . ." Do unto others! In a room full of PhDs I was revealing a third-grade sensibility.

"What does God mean to you?" Inasmuch as the last time I saw Him, He made me feel guilty what with all his complaints about readership and listenership, I said:

"God is guilt."

"God is guilt!" There was a lot of exchanging of glances around the room, so I must have said something very profound or very stupid and to this day I still don't know which.

"In your mind's eye, how do you imagine God to look?"

"In my eye's eye I can tell you He's nearly bald, He

has stooped shoulders, about five foot six, He has a Jewish nose and He overdresses.

"That is a remarkable image."

"Well, that's how He looks."

"Why do you say that?"

"Because I saw Him."

"You saw Him?"

I then revealed that I had actually *seen* God. This was something I hadn't told anybody yet. I knew my meeting with these gentlemen was coming up and I thought it might be better to let it come out in my discussions with them, rather than through another flashy press conference. It was a good decision, because that night when they issued a report on our initial progress, it included my statement that I had seen Him. So the press got the story anyway and in a much more credible setting. I was turning into a real media manipulator.

My new disclosure sent our discussion into a turmoil. As it was put by one of the professors, a rather stuffy organizational type from Princeton, "What we have claimed here is a *higher profile miracle.*"

They asked for time to discuss this new development and could I return the following day for further questioning. On my way back to the hotel, a remembrance from my childhood came to me, how in the Bronx where I grew up, a child claimed to have seen the Virgin Mary in a vacant lot and the lot was made into a local religious shrine and wouldn't it look ridiculous to make a religious shrine out of my hot-water heater?

I telephoned Judy, recounted the day's events, ordered a roast beef dinner, and then this deep metaphysical thinker watched a Jerry Lewis movie on television and went to sleep.

The next day, the scholars were gunning for me. They had asked an eminent "psycho-theologist," as they called him, to join their ranks, but it was apparent he was a shrink run in to check me out. I was getting my looney test after all. It's not enough to have your childhood God-notions examined, you have to endure some doctor observing what you do with your hands while talking. But it wouldn't look good, making a fuss over his being there, so I smiled wanly at Doctor Shrink, we'll call him, and we proceeded.

I was in there for five hours and I'm not going into all the rambling discourse that went on in that room—most of it had me restate things I had already said. But taken at random, some of the points covered in their search were: *God Is My Co-Pilot,* a World War II movie with Dennis Morgan; *The Song of Bernadette* with Jennifer Jones; *God Bless the Child,* the original Billie Holiday recording and the latter version by Blood, Sweat and Tears. There's nothing as self-indulgent as academicians in the open field. The details of my marriage. Reformed ceremony in a rabbi's study, followed by a brunch for the immediate family in The Rainbow Room. Somebody actually asked what we ate. Doctor Shrink went into the area of fantasy and dreams and did I ever "see" other people the way I claimed to have seen

74

God and I told him that I could distinguish between daydreams, night dreams, wet dreams and no dreams and that God actually sat in front of me, which was no dream. But he pressed on, making the point that a fantasy picture in the mind can have reality responses such as the mechanism that takes place in masturbation—and had I ever masturbated?—which got us into some of my adolescent masturbation fantasies over Jennifer Jones.

"Is that the same Jennifer Jones who played in *The Song of Bernadette?*" he asked.

"The same."

"A motion picture with a strong religious motif, is that not true?"

"Yes, but how is that relevant?"

"Only that we may have here the early beginnings of a distortion on your part of religious fantasy and sexual fantasy."

Now if this were true, it might have discredited me in the eyes of these esteemed scholars, a couple of whom were already blushing. But he wasn't going to pin any bum sex rap on me.

"It's an interesting theory, Doctor, but it won't work."

"How so?"

"I was doing it over Jennifer Jones as she appeared in *Ruby Gentry*—not *The Song of Bernadette.*

We drifted on. I don't know what kind of image I was projecting. It certainly wasn't that of a biblical expert.

"What is your favorite part of the Bible?"

"Ecclesiastes."

"Can you recite something?"

"To every thing, there is a season . . ." Except I didn't really know it and slipped into the lyrics of the Pete Seeger folk song adaptation and there were some embarrassed coughs for me, so I changed the subject by asking them if they wanted to hear "Shadrach, Meshach and Abed-nego" instead, and they didn't, and I didn't know it anyway.

I arrived on the third and final day of our meetings dreading another round of questioning. They informed me that they had already come to some definite conclusions based on our conversations. Their consensus was that I was a person with little or no philosophic or theological knowledge, that I had demonstrated over the years an astonishing lack of interest in spiritual matters, that God apparently held a place of marginal importance in my life—if that, and in general, they deemed me to be about the least qualified person in the world they could imagine speaking with God.

However, and it was a crucial qualifying however, the descriptions of my experience were so specific, so detailed, they found it difficult to conceive how I could have imagined it all, in the face of my obvious lack of interest in the subject.

What it came down to was—they didn't know. What I really think is they just didn't want to believe that unscholarly me could have spoken to God Himself, while they, who had spent their lifetimes in pursuit of God's

Truth, had to get it secondhand from such a moron.

Or maybe I'm not being fair. Maybe in the true scholarly tradition they just didn't feel they had enough documentation. And that was to be their statement. "We have not found sufficient documentation to support these claims." Clever wording. It doesn't say it didn't happen, just that there was no documentation.

Then they made a proposal based on what they said was a sense of fairness. They would wait until the following morning before issuing this statement, pending the arrival of certain evidence.

"What evidence?" I was speaking to the nominal chairman, the stuffy type from Princeton.

"We have prepared a set of questions for you to ask God."

"Oh, really? That's just terrific. Are they short answer or essay?"

"There are fifty questions."

"Fifty questions! You want me to get God to answer your fifty questions?"

"Included are many which have real historical and philosophical value to Mankind, so we would be compensating for the shallowness of your previous interviews."

"I notice you didn't say *alleged* interviews."

"Until tomorrow morning we are operating on the assumption your story is true."

"Thanks."

"We'll know soon enough if you're fabricating. Unless

77

you are concealing an abundant knowledge, which we doubt, there are questions here you could not possibly answer by remaining in your hotel room until tomorrow. That will be our control factor."

"Lovely. And I just go back there and get God to perform His number—and then I show up with the answers in the morning."

"It might be difficult for you. It couldn't be difficult for Him."

"How do I reach Him? Call Room Service?"

Then they handed over their questions in a manila envelope and the court of inquiry was over. As I made my way out of the building, Doctor Shrink ran up to me.

"I just wanted to say I had to be here in a professional capacity. But as a private opinion, let me offer that—if this is not true, sir, I think you are in need of help."

"No kidding?"

I went back to the hotel and called New York.

"Yes, Judy, fifty questions."

"What will you do?"

"I'd like to do a Moses." But how could I summon God? He summons you.

"Forget it," she said. "You went down there because it might help, and if it doesn't, so what? Let them make their statement."

"It could be gorgeous, though—"

"What?"

"If I went back there tomorrow with His answers."

78

"Honey, come home."

"Tomorrow."

I said goodbye to Judy, then I lay back on my bed in my room at The Georgetown Inn, and with the *chutzpa* of all time, I tried to summon God.

"Hello, God?"

Hello, God—out loud like that. It sounded pretty foolish, especially when there was a knock on the door and I realized somebody was out there and overheard me.

"Room Service."

I opened the door and there He was, God, wearing a bellhop's uniform and pushing a tray of tea and cookies.

"Hello, cutie," He said.

I was dumbfounded.

"So let me in." He came into the room and I closed the door behind Him.

"Someday this will go down in history," He said, "as the Miracle of the Tea and Cookies."

"You came! I summoned God!"

"So I came. Don't make a big deal. Here, oatmeal cookies, your favorite."

Do you think He baked them Himself?

"They gave you some grilling, those fellas."

"That's their job. God is their profession."

"So why are you fooling around with them? TV, I keep telling you. That's got the impact."

"I decided you have to touch all the bases."

"By me, you're stranded at second base."

"But you came. Does that mean you'll help?"

"Why I came is to tell you, enough of this. Every night I watch Johnny Carson and no you."

"I'm sorry."

"Don't be sorry. Just do it. And don't get so guilty. God is guilt! Such a thing. So let me see those questions."

He sat back in the chair to look them over, removing his little red-and-black bellhop's cap to be comfortable, and I don't know how people are going to feel about this, particularly if it's their belief that God is ultimate and perfect, but He took out a pair of bifocals to help Him read better.

"*Oy-oy-oy!* Such a *tsimmes.*"

I looked over His shoulder.

"What is that?"

"What that is—is so you shouldn't make up a story. A control factor, they said. I'll say. It is fifty questions all right and it is written in Aramaic. And I know you don't know Aramaic, because you didn't even do so hot with Hebrew."

"Those bastards. Excuse me."

"It's okay. They pulled on you a peppy trick. You send a fella to college, he has to show off."

I looked at the paper. It was absolutely impenetrable. God was reading, moving His lips while He read.

"To tell you the truth, my Aramaic is a little rusty. Such questions. Look at this. 'What is the true origin of the Universe?' 'What is the source of the planet Earth?'

80

'Establish the date of the Creation.' What is this, a history final?"

He thought a moment then He said, "I don't know. You really want this?"

"If it's not too much trouble."

"From this, you'd really impress them. Impress them? They'd *plotz*." He thumbed through the questions again. "Well, so long as I'm here, we can give a fast run-through. But listen, use a typewriter. Your handwriting is terrible."

And that is what we did. God dictated the questions and the answers, and here is part of it:

" 'Did Man fall from Grace with Adam?' You talk about Adam, I'll tell you something that never came out. I made not such a smart decision there. I made Adam seventeen and Eve sixteen. A couple of teenagers running around naked in the woods. Hippies! Anything could have happened.

" 'Which of the world's religions is closest to the Divine Truth?' I should get into preferences? All of them are cute.

" 'Is Jesus Christ the son of God?' Jesus was a nice fella." I think He really wanted to leave it at that, but possibly the look of indecision on my face led Him to go on. "Well, the thing is, people who want to believe that Jesus was my son can go ahead and believe it. It's what they want to think and I don't get into that. I mean, I created the Universe, I didn't create Religion. Jesus was my son. Buddha was my son. Confucius. Mohammed.

81

Moses. All the fellas. All God's chillun are my chillun, if you know what I mean.

" 'What is the true meaning of Man's existence?' This is like Philosophy 101. Life is a fountain! No, on this I have to say Man's existence means what you think it means and what I think doesn't count. How's that for a deepy?

" 'What is your position on abortion?' A committee asks questions, this is what you get. And this is just what I'm talking about, on looking to God. You can't work this out for yourselves? My position on abortion! This is like Meet the Press.

" 'Will there be a Judgment Day for Man—if so, when?' What do they want, a date to mark down on a calendar? First of all, I don't do judgments. I just don't get into that. And if they mean a Doomsday, end-of-the-world thing, I'm certainly not going to get into that. That's for you to decide, but if you want my personal opinion, I wouldn't look forward to it because there would be a lot of yelling and screaming and who needs that? Also I wouldn't be doing anything like sitting up on a big throne saying who goes to Heaven and who goes to Hell because it would look silly, people going past me like a Radio City production number.

" 'Why have you chosen to appear at this time?' This I told my fella in the first interview—that I'm here to say I built into what you got, everything you need to make it work, and I think if you know this to be a fact it could help you a little."

And so it went. He was careful not to commit Himself on specifics, leaving most questions for Man to decide. He wouldn't take sides on religious questions. And He was, at all times, very colloquial. He even had something to say about that at the end.

"Listen, I want to say that I hope nobody gets offended from my manner of talking. This was chosen originally to fit the fella who I picked out to talk to because he was a contemporary fella—and it just so happened he was a Jewish fella from New York. Likewise if I look to him to be Jewish, it's for the same reason, and nobody should be offended because I'm no more Jewish than I am anything else. Also I don't mean to take all these fancy questions from important scholars and give back snappy answers. The big thing is not *how* I say it, but *what* I'm saying and I think I can communicate with more people by talking this way than with fancy words like 'cosmological' and 'ontological,' which believe you me I know how to use. So what I'm really saying to the world is: I'm here and it can work and I root for you and I like you a lot and try not to hurt each other."

10

IF I HAD any desire to be smug the next day when I handed over the answers, I'm glad I repressed it. My arrival with those typed pages caused such a look of surprise on the faces of those men, it was almost poignant. A couple of them took to crossing themselves, the professor from Southern Methodist, a frail little man, looked like he was about to faint, while the stuffed shirt from Princeton just glared, enraged no doubt.

They said they would certainly need some time to go

over the material and in what had to be a small victory, they all got up and saw me to the door, down the hall, down the University steps, across the green and out the gate. I looked back as I was about to turn a corner and disappear out of sight, and they were all still standing at the gate, watching me.

When I got home, Judy filled me in on the waves I had made with the statement about my basement encounter with God. The press had been calling—could they see where it happened?—and we arranged a press tour of my basement. "This is the light switch, these are the steps, this is the hot-water heater, this is the paint can, this is the fuse box . . ." The following day, a wire-service photo of my basement appeared in nearly every paper in the country.

Remember those puzzles on the backs of breakfast food boxes—how many rabbits can you see in this picture? Well, 106 people from coast to coast called their local newspapers to say they had actually seen God standing next to the heater in their newspaper pictures.

There was resentment, too, over the fact that I said God looked Jewish.

"Couldn't you have said He looked average, Middle American?" Judy asked.

"But He didn't."

"And you had to say He had a Jewish nose."

"That's what He had."

"What's the difference between a Jewish nose, an Italian nose, and an Armenian nose?"

"The nose."

Judy felt that to a lot of non-Jewish people I was saying God *is* Jewish. I pointed out that even He was on record on the subject, which would come out of the Georgetown report.

"Nobody knows that yet."

"They will soon enough when the group releases it."

"Yes, people will love that you said He served you oatmeal cookies."

"That's not in the record."

"And His voice. Why couldn't you say He sounded like a radio announcer? They're always straight, down-the-middle voices."

"Honey, with His voice He couldn't have gotten on WEVD."

WEVD is the Yiddish-American station in New York and to be accurate about it, they actually have terrific sounding voices.

True to Judy's instincts, we started getting some crazy calls. It tallied out to something like eight "Jew Bastards," five "Dirty Jews," six "Kike Commies," and one obscene breather who slipped in there somehow. We decided to change our phone to an unlisted number with a twenty-four-hour answering service and I imagined somebody getting the number anyway and the answering service lady saying, "Yes, I'll tell him. He's a commie-homo-bastard. Thank you for calling."

There were some hate letters calling me a fagit, fakkit and faggid and a few that didn't get commie right either. And some hate telegrams, a new product of our electronic age. Western Union won't accept malicious wording in a telegram, but what obviously started out as "Drop Dead, Jew!" got through as "Wishing you discomfort in your Jewishness," and what was probably intended as a curt "You Jew!" arrived as "You are a Jewish person."

In an open field outside of Battle Creek, Michigan, 5,000 Seventh-Day Adventists held a candlelight vigil to refute my claims and pray for me.

In Chicago, a 51-year-old housewife claimed she saw God in *her* basement, the reporting of which set off a chain of other miracles, with God allegedly appearing in five basements, two garages, six kitchens, fourteen bedrooms—do you think there *is* a sexual connection there?—and three ceilings.

My believability must have been on the upswing, though, and I know this is a perverse statistic, but even so, twelve hallucinators saw God exactly as I first described Him, Nehru suit and all. I wondered if He could have actually appeared to any of these people, but when I asked Him He said, "What do you think, I have nothing better to do than *shlep* in and out of basements like a plumber?"

I was asked to do an interview at home for CBS-TV News and Mike Wallace walked through the basement with me, bringing an NBC and ABC request to do the same with—as I had been cautiously dubbed by the journalists—"The Alleged God-Seer," "The Man Who

Says He Saw God," and my favorite, "The Miracle Claimant."

We arranged for me to appear on The Flip Wilson Show and I knew that would make God happy. But it brought out a lot of my repressed desires to be a performer, stemming back to my all too brief solo in the song "Dry Bones" for the DeWitt Clinton High School Chorus, and numerous neurotic moments doing impersonations of Johnny Mathis and Tony Bennett at the teenage parties of my life. For a brief instant I imagined what it would be like to stand out there and do something, like my Tony Bennett. "Because of you, there's a song in my heart . . ."

The moment came and Flip Wilson said, in a bastardization of even the cautious appellation of the journalists: "We have a special guest tonight in our studio audience, the alleged man who says he claims to have seen God." And I stood up and waved to everybody and sat down. I never got to sing.

God said do Johnny Carson, so Johnny Carson was next. I talked to the producer by phone only he wasn't going to give me as much exclusivity on the show as I hoped. He explained, after all, they have a widely varied audience and a need for "stars" in the show business sense, and as I was a controversial figure to boot, they had to work around me, so I was booked to appear with Tom Seaver, Raquel Welch and Peggy Lee.

Going on one of these shows has a strange quality because you sit backstage in a room waiting to go on,

88

watching a television set which carries the program as it's being taped at that moment and it feels like you're watching TV at home, only you're not watching at home, you *are* the show. Then you go out, do your appearance, and because it is taped you can go home and watch yourself. It's strange. Anyway, Raquel Welch plugged her latest movie, Peggy Lee plugged her latest song, Tom Seaver plugged his latest book, Johnny and Ed plugged their sponsors' products, and I went out to plug God.

Carson was nervous. So much of his audience is out in the heartland, you just knew he didn't want to offend them. This probably accounted for my going on so late in the show, what would be about 12:45 A.M., New York time. His staff had prepared a set of questions on index cards, and I thought that at this stage I probably could have index cards of my own with the set answers, so routine had getting interviewed become. And it was routine until I said,

"Yes, Johnny, I'm here to say I saw God," which brought a lady to her feet in the back shouting,

"God lives! He is alive, in living color."

Later that night, when the show was aired, this was bleeped out, as well as the sight of the woman being carried from the studio screaming, "God lives on NBC!"

Carson, who had turned pale, managed to get off a quip to me, "Can't take you anywhere," and called for a station break to restore order in the studio. Trying to be humorous myself, off mike I said to him that they could

89

use the woman's "God lives on NBC!" as a station break, but he didn't think that was very funny.

During the break Carson went off to confer with his staff, Ed McMahon did a commercial for a product that cleans out stuffed drains, and Raquel Welch leaned over to say that I was a very interesting person.

Carson came back with new resolve to finish the show and before we went back on, asked me if I'd be willing to submit to a little experiment his production staff had cooked up. They had brought down a police artist, the kind of person who specializes in drawing faces from eyewitness descriptions. They thought it would make for good television if I could talk the artist through a sketch of God, as I claimed to have seen Him. It sounded imaginative to me and I agreed. Carson explained to his audience what we were going to do. Then the artist came out and on camera began to sketch the face as I described it, making adjustments along the way—"Eyes a little closer together, mouth a little weaker, etc." He worked very fast and it was remarkable. If you've ever seen any of these before-and-after drawings when they capture a suspect—the artists may not get it precisely right, but they do get a feeling of the face, and he was getting it. I could see we were just about running out of air time when Carson said:

"We'll be back to look at the final result after this word from Ed." From Ed we got the news of a new paper towel and then we were back to God. The finished result was not photographically perfect, but it did have something of the sense of Him.

"Yes, that looks a lot like God as I saw Him."

The camera came in for a closeup of the sketch, they pressed the Applause sign for the studio audience, but somebody started shouting, "No, no, liar!" the audience was buzzing, there were a couple of boos, an old lady fainted, and The Tonight Show was out of time and off the air.

Carson stepped forward and asked his audience to please calm down and they did except for grumblings from some offended people who looked like they wanted to hit me, as opposed to the ladies who wanted to touch me or the girls who wanted my autograph or the vast majority who were probably more upset that Peggy Lee didn't have time to sing another song.

The producer of the show came up with a uniformed guard and said it would be better if the guard saw me to a cab, considering the excitement in the studio, and he led me out a side door. He hailed a cab and I got in, still shaken by the boffo ending to the show.

I sat down, too preoccupied to notice the driver of the cab. It was God. He was wearing a cap, a plaid jacket and He had a little black cigar stub sticking out of his mouth.

"So. The Johnny Carson Show. Finally."

"You have a way of startling me."

"Sorry, but for me, it's very easy to be dramatic." He

chewed on His cigar. "I'll tell you, I didn't love how it went," He said.

"Well, there was a little excitement at the end."

"What was with that drawing thing?"

"It sounded like a good idea."

"Cops and robbers he plays with God."

"What do you mean?"

"An artist who draws crooks. He makes everybody look like a crook. He made me look like a second-story man."

I happened to notice the dashboard. As part of His gestalt, He had a hack license with His photograph and the name, GOD typed out.

"I want you should do more television," He said, "and no more drawings and no more with the going on for the last fifteen minutes—that's for fellas who write diet books."

We reached the house and I was about to get out of the cab when I saw that He'd been running the meter.

"Do I pay you?"

"What do you think?"

I didn't know. I waited for a reaction from Him, but He just looked at me. The meter read $1.10. Tentatively, I handed Him a dollar and a quarter and He took it. So I said,

"Keep the change."

And He said, "Thanks, bud."

I had just given God a tip! And He accepted. Then He burst out laughing.

"Here. Take your money back. I was just kidding. A little joke."

And He drove off, chuckling to Himself all the way. It led me to a philosophic observation. I decided that one of the things Man doesn't need in this Universe is for God to have a sense of humor, especially a lousy one.

11

JUDY hadn't accompanied me to the taping because she was at home, preparing for a little dinner party. It was with friends whom we had been ignoring during the excitement of the last few weeks. Elaine and Lester Hirsh were already there when I arrived and the plan was for us to have drinks, eat, and then because it was inevitable, we would all watch me with Johnny Carson.

We each brought to the watching of the show something of our own personalities and when it was over, we

94

all had different responses. Judy thought it was wonderful and that the artist's drawing was a great publicity idea. Elaine, who is a shy person, couldn't get over my sitting there in front of so many people. Lester, who is my attorney and a practical person, was intrigued with the number of commercials on the show. And I, who am a person whose hair is thinning, thought I looked bald.

Seeing God puts demands on your friends. They really don't know what to say. Elaine kept going to the fact of what a celebrity I was becoming, while Lester asked a lot of questions about how much I got paid, and do you have to join the union to go on television.

"Yes, that's all interesting, but do you believe I met God?"

They looked at each other for support. Desperately, Elaine turned to Judy.

"Do you, Judy?"

Judy had made her separate peace. She also had her pat answer: "I believe he believes, which is the same as believing."

"That's good enough for me," Elaine said. "I believe Judy believes that you believe, which is the same as believing."

"I think it's getting a bit removed," I said. "What about you, Lester?"

"I believe Elaine believes that Judy believes . . ."

"No, come on, a straight answer."

"I don't really know. But I would defend your right to say what you believe—and I may have to."

"What do you mean?" Judy asked.

"I'm just kidding."

"Lester always sees the dark side," Elaine said. "It's either because he's a lawyer, or he's a lawyer because of it, but he always sees the terrible consequences of every situation."

"What terrible consequences?" Judy asked.

"Go on, Lester," I said.

"Well, let us assume that the lady who fainted at the end died, or was permanently hospitalized . . . let us just say . . ." Don't you just love lawyers? ". . . if this poor old lady brought a suit against you claiming that her death or permanent hospitalization was caused by you—that's really reaching—but you could become involved."

"Yes, that's really reaching," I said.

"But it could tie up your time. That's what a lot of stupid lawsuits do."

"What else could happen?" Judy asked.

"*Two* old ladies could die or become permanently hospitalized," I said.

"You could be sued for character assassination."

"By?"

"By members of God's immediate family."

"So nothing could happen."

"It wouldn't hold up, but you could be sued by every church in the country on the grounds that your remarks eroded confidence in the church and cost them contributions."

96

"Feel better, honey? Lester is telling us I have a perfect legal right to see God."

I was wrong. Lester's idle cocktail party speculations that night were to have very real applications. It began with a decision by the publicity department of The Tonight Show. Television shows want publicity and publicity departments are in the business of doing it, so they released to the press an eight-by-ten-inch glossy photograph of the police artist's rendering of God along with a press release giving the background of the drawing. It was picked up by everybody—the wire services, newspapers, television news programs. The next day, you couldn't look at a news source without seeing that drawing.

```
"Is this God's face?"
"God, from the miracle claimant's view"
"Alleged God-seer's alleged God"
```

It brought forth some of the loudest, most virulent attacks on me of any incident in the entire controversy. This time I had gone too far, I had created a graven image, had cheapened Him, was un-American—I don't know how they got to that—and was a menace to God-loving, God-fearing people everywhere.

Well, we live in an open society, we are told, and there is free speech and if nothing else I was in my legal right of free speech to say whatever I chose on this subject, so you would think.

Well, one night—incidentally, this has nothing to do

with what happened, I just include it to demonstrate how little the average person, in this case, me, knows about his rights under the law—one night, Judy and I go into a midtown pizzeria and the pizza we order comes out cold and oily and terrible, and I try to send it back, but the waiter is afraid of the chef and won't take it back and says I should go into the kitchen myself and argue with the chef, and I say bring the manager and the waiter says the manager isn't there, and the chef won't come out, and we won't eat the pizza and I'm not going to pay for it. So we get up and walk out of the restaurant, whereby the waiter, wearing his red waiter's outfit, follows us into the street walking alongside of us, yelling and waving the check in our faces, down crowded Broadway, with people stopping to watch us, and the waiter calls a policeman who makes us go back to the restaurant, and the manager magically appears and says forget it, and what we did wrong, according to Lester, is leave the restaurant because there was a contract which we broke by not paying the check, and if I'm not certain how the law works pertaining to pizzas, how would I possibly know about the provisions of the New York State Mental Hygiene Law?

So, getting back to what happened, the man's name was Owen D. Shallimar, Jr., a conservative, wealthy, God-fearing, God-loving man, a former corporation counsel, who in his twilight years handled real estate deals in Newport, R. I., where he lived, keeping a token apartment on Park Avenue in a building which he

98

owned. I had offended him. Outspoken I. Jewish I. Godless I. Somehow he had me Jewish and Godless. Unkempt in appearance I. Have I mentioned yet that I have a moustache and sideburns? I have a moustache and sideburns, an obvious compensation for my previously referred to thinning hair. It was a classic matchup of the old world, White Anglo-Saxon Protestant versus the Balding Immigrant.

With a nod to Bob Dylan, I tell you we both felt we had God on Our Side. Actually, I had God. Shallimar had The Law.

The Law appeared in the form of Officers Vincent T. Sabatello and John F. G. Kearney of the 13th Precinct who came to my apartment with little American flags in their lapels. They had come to answer the complaint of Mr. Owen D. Shallimar, Jr., that I was "a dangerous lunatic capable of doing injury to himself or others" as it was read aloud to me by Officer Sabatello.

"Well, as you can see, I'm just a peaceful person at home with my wife."

"Are you the same individual who appeared last night on Johnny Carson, said appearance causing immediate disturbance in the studio audience, as reported in today's edition of the *New York Daily News?*"

"That is not exactly what happened."

"Are you the same individual who has been appearing publicly and making public statements saying that you have seen and spoken to God?"

"Yes, but surely there is no law against that."

99

"Are you the same individual who caused a lady to be carried screaming from the studio of the aforementioned Johnny Carson Show, as also was reported in the *New York Daily News?*"

"She was a crazy lady—"

"Now just one minute, Officer. My husband does not have to submit to any questions."

"Is your husband the same individual who has been said to be acting psycho and who claimed God talked to him in his basement, causing hystericalness . . ."—at this point Officer Sabatello paused to look in his notebook—"in one lady, Miss Jane R. Foster of Flushing, Queens, who is now in a state mental hospital for observation?"

"What is this, Kafka? Are you charging me with a crime?"

"Are you the same individual who caused a crowd to collect after the Johnny Carson show last night and in said crowd that you caused to be collected, an argument ensued and one Robert R. Basehart of the Bronx was struck with a fist and suffered minor contusions?"

"I don't know anything about that—and I want you out of this house!" I was getting pretty damned mad and we were squared off chin to chin.

"Do you claim you have seen and spoken to God?"

"I don't have to answer these questions."

"He doesn't have to answer anything. I'm calling our lawyer." Judy went toward the phone and reactively

Officer Kearney moved with her movements, seeming to step in her way.

"Don't you threaten my wife!"

"Don't become violent," said Officer Kearney, his hand on his revolver.

"I want you two fascists out of here!" Not the smartest thing to say.

I pushed my way past Officer Kearney to get to the phone, bumping into him in the process, he responding by grabbing my arm with a "Now listen here—" I responding by trying to pull my arm back, he responding by not wanting to give it back to me, and with Officer Kearney tugging at me and me tugging back, I somehow managed to reach the phone and dial Lester's number and I got his answering service.

I was really furious now. "Get out of here or I'll call the police!"

"We are the police."

"I know that. I'm trying irony on you, you galoots."

"Doesn't know who the police is."

"You have no right to be here," Judy screamed.

"Out!" As I firmly took Officer Sabatello by the arm and forcefully guided him toward the door. Lesson learned. Never put your hands on a cop.

"I think he's becoming dangerous by virtue of his mental condition," said Officer Sabatello to Officer Kearney, while grabbing my arms and pinning them behind my back.

"Is the public safety at stake?" said Kearney to Sabatello.

I howled, "Let go of me. This is not Nazi Germany!"

"Where *do* you think you are? Can you tell us that?"

"What do you mean, can I tell you that? This is my home and you're in it and I want you out of it and release me and release my wife!" Officer Kearney having embraced my screaming, kicking wife in a bear hug.

"We are here to answer a complaint by Owen D. Shallimar, Jr." And who the hell was he and why the hell was that officer bodily restraining my wife and this officer holding me, and if two cops come into your house, asking questions, bumping you, accusing you, refusing to leave and ultimately wrestling with you, physically touching you and your loved one, what you might do is get so angry you wriggle free and kick one of them hard in the shins and try to pull his badge off his uniform, remembering in your anger that in a dispute it's good to get the officer's badge number, and there, after all, is his whole badge? And if one of the cops calls for reinforcements and in what seems like seconds the room is filled with cops, and you're screaming, fighting mad at this incredible intrusion, and if the more you rage and pull away from them, the more it reinforces what they came to check out, which is that you are a violent person, and if one of the officers tries to handcuff you to your own radiator pipe and you attempt to make a small political point about Fascism by pulling his American flag off his lapel—then what could happen is that your

102

wife is reduced to a bewildered creature not believing that her husband is actually being arrested, actually being informed of his rights while being deprived of his rights, actually being told that for the good of the public safety he is being detained, actually being placed in a straitjacket and actually being taken off to Bellevue in a police van for observation. Yes, that's right. Arrested. Straitjacket. Bellevue.

Of course, afterward lawyer Hirsh would point out, citing *Warner v. The State of New York,* that an officer has the power under common law to arrest and detain the mentally ill—guess who that allegedly was?—to prevent the party from doing injury to himself or to others, and any peace officer may take that apparently mentally ill person into custody, based on his appraisal of the situation, arrest you, straitjacket you, paddy-wagon you, Bellevue you—and do people know that, people who are in the same pizza-pie category as me?

I was riding along in the back of the van like a criminal, I, who had only recently been in direct communication with The Lord God. Suddenly, like dawn breaking over the roof of Bellevue, it occurred to me that the more I had protested, the more I had confirmed their preconceived opinion of me. So in the great tradition of the Count of Monte Cristo and the Birdman of Alcatraz, I decided to outwit my captors.

I would protest no further, give them no more crazy-person documentation for them to wink knowingly about. However, you would think that if you protested strongly and that made them think you were a crazy person, then if you acted passively it would convince them you were not. But it only made them suspect you even more, because how come you're acting passively under the circumstances, and you still must be a crazy person. It's sort of like Catch-23.

So much for my strategy. I knew that at that very moment Judy would be in touch with Lester to obtain my release. All I would have to worry about was whether or not to sue for false arrest. Listen to me—The Bellevue Lawyer.

What I didn't know was that Judy was mad out of her mind simply trying to find Lester, and if not Lester, any other attorney. Elaine didn't know where Lester was, in court, she thought, but when Judy asked if Elaine could give her the name of somebody else, Elaine said that Lester would be very offended if I had done anything as colorful as getting committed without giving him a crack at it.

Judy called the lawyer at the company she'd previously worked for. He didn't want to get involved, he said, but he told Judy, free of charge, that what she needed was a court order from a judge of the Supreme Court—and how could she get that? Through a lawyer. He did give her the names of some lawyers, all of whom were out of town, in court, or in conference. You wouldn't think it would be such a hassle to get a lawyer in his office and at his desk, but try it some time, preferably not when your mate has just been carted off to the booby hatch. She was about to dial anybody at all out of the Yellow Pages when she remembered that my play agent retained a lawyer and she called my agent, but my agent, as is the custom of agents who represent playwrights who have unsold plays and who might be receiving a call that had something to do with the business of their doing their job of selling the plays, had her secretary tell Judy she was out to lunch, which was a pretty automatic response, considering it was nearly 6 P.M.

On a hunch, Judy called the tennis courts at Central Park, the spot at which all the lawyers, doctors and analysts you couldn't reach if you were desperate were convening, and there indeed was our Lester. I'll say this for him, he did break off his game, stranding the other lawyer. But there was no way of his getting my release. I was being formally and legally held for observation and that was that. The best he could do was get me scheduled to appear before a judge the following day, which he did. Meantime, I was in custody and had to undergo the indignity of an enforced psychiatric examination by two doctors at Bellevue.

The procedure is a lot like every movie you've ever seen on the subject and while it's happening to you, you're saying, I saw this movie, only it's not a movie and it's happening to you.

The most important thing about it is that these doctors have seen them all. The wilder your story, the more logical it becomes for them to accept it in their usual context, that of having seen all these crackpots. So if a fellow comes in who is supposed to have met with God, they have this terrific overview. They've seen you before.

"You've met with God? That's nice?"

Yes, once you enter the circle of the crazies, it's very hard to get out, as it was becoming clear to me. So I started relying on as much name-dropping as I could muster, throwing a lot of "As reported in *The New York Times*-es" into my answers. It didn't seem to impress them. They had absolutely no outward reaction to anything you said. They just wrote it down. You got the feeling you could say anything and they would just write it down. There was this perverse temptation to do just that, just to see them *not* respond. "I can fly." And they would write down: "He can fly." "I am a zebra." "He is a zebra." I fought off that temptation, though. I was having enough trouble with the basic line of questioning.

"How many times have you seen God?"

"I've actually *seen* Him three times. Twice we spoke by intercom."

"Seen God three times, spoke twice by intercom," they write down.

"Does He appear to you in different shapes?"

"Same shape. Different outfits."

"Different outfits?"

"Yes. He seems to have a flexible wardrobe." It was

106

impossible. There was just no way I could relate it all in that place to those doctors and make it sound believable. Some of the questions didn't help either.

"Does God ever appear to you as a beautiful woman?"

"What kind of sick question is that?"

"Please answer the question."

"No. Just as a little old fella." Writes down, "Little old fella."

They had me in that room for four hours, cataloguing every minute detail of my meetings with Him, running me through physical tests and mental tests, these two incredibly dry, humorless men, whom I wouldn't want to meet at a party.

"Look at this." It was a Rorschach. "What do you see?"

"A corned beef on rye and a side of potato salad."

I was famished, but at Bellevue there's no sending out for a sandwich from the Stage Delicatessen. Doctor Browder, the dull man of about fifty of the team, not to be confused with Doctor Hauptman, the dull man of about fifty, phoned for dinner to be brought to me. It arrived on a plastic tray, canned string beans, mashed potatoes and a piece of some mystery fish. Since it was their custom to observe everything I did in that room, they also took notes on how I ate the fish. I ate it tentatively.

Finally, it appeared as though they were finished.

Doctor Browder thanked Doctor Hauptman—you'd think they'd thank me—and called for an aide to come for me.

"I'm told your lawyer has a court order for you to appear before a judge tomorrow morning at ten."

"Then I'm free to go?" His response was to write down my remark.

"And your wife says she loves you." That really lost something in the translation.

"Do you know if God called?" Trying for a little sarcasm after four hours with The Twin Doctors. Their response was to write that down also.

"Might I know your verdict?"

"You'll be given a bed for the night with clean sheets."

"That's an odd answer to my question."

"I think that does it, Doctor."

"Yes, Doctor."

That's the way they talked to each other, calling each other "Doctor." My buddies nodded a doctor's goodbye to me and left.

A policeman and a big hospital orderly came for me. They took me to a ward where there were four men, all fast asleep, two of them strapped to their beds. It wasn't exactly a group house on Fire Island.

The orderly didn't have anything to say to me but:

"Make any trouble and we'll tie you up." I didn't feel there was much to negotiate on that.

A nurse came by and wanted me to take a sleeping

pill, but nobody was going to conk me out. If I was going to spend the night in the psychiatric ward at Bellevue, it was going to be with all my faculties and wide awake.

The bed to my left was vacant. To my right was a man of about forty with a crew cut. He was moaning. This was going to be some night. His moaning kept getting louder and louder. Then he suddenly sat straight up in his bed, wide awake, and looked at me.

"Ask me why I'm moaning."

"Huh?"

"Ask me why I'm moaning. You got the bed next to a guy who's moaning and you don't ask him why he's moaning?"

"Why are you moaning?"

"The state of the world is heavy on my shoulders."

"I'm sorry."

"Ask me why the state of the world is heavy on my shoulders."

"Look, mister, let me—"

"Cutting me off? You don't cut me off. Do you know who I am?"

"Good night now—"

"I am God!"

Wonderful. Somebody in the hospital thought it would be cute to put the guy who thinks he *met* God in with the guy who thinks he *is* God."

"You're God. That's very good."

"Don't humor me. God knows when you humor Him."

"Yes, that's true."

"Doing it again! You think I'm crazy and you can humor me. But *you're* the crazy one. You think you've seen God."

"How do you know that?"

"I know. And even if I didn't know—the nurse told me."

"Well, I *did* see God." I was actually arguing with him.

"But you didn't see *me*. You don't believe I'm God, do you?"

"I'm going to sleep now—"

"I'll show you. I know everything. Ask me any question."

"You go to sleep, okay?"

"Ask me any question. If you don't ask me any question, I'll keep you up all night."

"Look, I'm going to call the nurse."

"And then what? She thinks you're crazy, too. Ask me any question."

"Now look here—"

"Ask me, ask me."

"Oh, dammit. Who was the center fielder for the Washington Senators in 1945?"

"Bingo Binks."

"What?"

"Bingo Binks! That's the answer! People are crazy—they always ask you sports. Sports and geography. No imagination."

110

"You are very smart."

"Humoring me again. You know, you're crazy. Want to know how I know?"

"How do you know?"

"I know everything. Ask me a question."

"How do I get you to be quiet?"

"Hey, that was very clever. You get me to be quiet by saying, 'Good night, God.' "

"Good night, God."

"Hear what you just said? Now doesn't that make you feel crazy?"

Delighted with himself, he turned over and chuckled himself to sleep. He slept through the night, except for one time when he sat straight up and said, "Will the real God please stand up?" and then he chuckled himself to sleep again.

Poor guy. That I was considered suitable to occupy the next bed from that unfortunate fruitcake was a fact I had no intention of accepting. I just lay there, awake all night, reviewing my life. They did a Fellini march in front of me, like that last scene in 8½—family, friends, old girlfriends, all showed up in Bellevue to say hello and tell me it would turn out all right, because I had found my calling—I was a Chosen Person. Clearly, in this crisis situation I had adopted the attitude that it wasn't really a crisis situation. And with my firm grasp of the Law—see *Pizza Pie*—I didn't know that the judge, if he felt I needed mental care, could hold me for thirty days of observation, after which time I could be

111

sent to a state mental hospital for treatment for a six-month period, with various options to renew, all options on their side. Of course, in my self-deceived Chosen Person Mystique, I half expected I wouldn't even stay the night. God would steal into the ward like Peter Pan and take me home.

He never showed up.

12

THE following morning, looking like a mess from lack of sleep, I was taken by handcuff, taken in chains! from the hospital to the courtroom.

As I stepped out of the building, the press was waiting. They had missed the sight of me being brought in. They certainly weren't going to miss me coming out. The cumulative power of the press is wonderful when it's working for you, but when it turns the other way, well, some time ago there was that kid, Michael J.

Brody, who was going to give away millions. The press was all over him, they covered every move he made, he got a recording contract, sang on Ed Sullivan, the works. Weeks later, the word got out on the wire services that he had been arrested and was being held for psychiatric examination. Just the words, "psychiatric examination" were enough to do him in as far as the press was concerned. They were finished with him, and as a result, so was the public. It didn't even matter if the charges were valid. And now I was being held for psychiatric examination. What would it do to my credibility?

"SAW GOD, SEES DOCTORS" said the ungracious *Daily News*.

The *paparazzi* jumped at me. I've never been confronted by the legendary European *paparazzi*, but the group outside Bellevue had several civilians among the pros. They were Japanese tourists with Nikons and American tourists with Polaroids who had drifted a few blocks east from their regular rounds of the Empire State Building. My sanity had become a tourist attraction.

The pros did their job. By the next day, all America was treated to the sight of messy, handcuffed me, framed against the hallowed halls of Bellevue. The Michael J. Brody Effect was in effect. And I didn't even get to sing on Network TV. As you can see, even from my recollection of it, I was being fairly casual because I just didn't realize I was actually on the brink of being

114

put away for a long, long time, long after the point when I would have dropped off the chart of the media's Top 100 Hits.

I later learned that the photographers being on the scene at the precise time of my emergence from the hospital was the handiwork of Owen D. Shallimar, Jr. I remember when most public relations and advertising in this country was run by tough, conservative Old Ivy types like him. Then the Greeks and the Italians and the Jews moved into those fields and all the Greeks and the Italians and the Jews forgot those Old Ivy guys had been there before them. I got a reminder. Shallimar had skillfully arranged for the press to be there when I came out, even held a little sidewalk press conference before they led me out, saying he was going to expose to all the world the sadness of my mental state. And then, timed beautifully, out I stride, attached to a cop, emerging from the nuthouse. He couldn't have played it better.

Judy and Lester rushed up to me. I assured Judy I was all right, something Lester seemed to disagree with.

"You're in a lot of trouble."

"What kind of judicial restraint is that?"

"Well, we'll try."

"You'll try? You'll do more than try!"

"Shh. Don't raise your voice. Act normal. Especially now."

"Listen here, Lester."

"Not too loud. Your accuser is watching you."

There was Shallimar, looking very pleased with himself, a tall, muscular man, who looked as though he never had to shave, and in what was one of the more ominous signs to me, he had his hair parted down the middle. I turned toward him, I don't know what I was going to say exactly, but as I turned, he recoiled in the style of John Barrymore. Off went the cameras, and as a follow-up picture to the story, America saw crazy me apparently threatening meek and defenseless Owen D. Shallimar, Jr. If you ever have any public relations to do, don't overlook the old-time heavy hitters.

The friendly policeman pushed me toward the waiting van and we were off to see the wizard. My personal van pulled away from the curb, followed by Lester and Judy in Lester's car, followed by Shallimar in his chauffeur-driven Bentley, followed by the press in station wagons and taxicabs. It wasn't the circumstances you'd want, but I had my first motorcade.

They took me to the chamber of New York State Supreme Court Justice Richard G. Levine, pronounce "Lavyne." I have always mistrusted Levines pronounced Lavyne and Shapiros pronounced Shapyro. Apart from being pretentious, it's a bit nit-picky. Judge Levine was both of these things. In a grand manner, he informed both sides that in this hearing he would call the shots, and that it was not to be a carnival for the press, either, and the public would be barred. I wasn't sure if that would work for me or against me, but having already been outhit by Owen D., I guessed I was better off.

"Counselor Shallimar, you have brought the petition

and it will be for you to establish the mental incompetence of the defendant. You may call witnesses and present evidence accordingly."

Shallimar then handed over just like that a folder on me three inches thick. I had a sudden loathing for Xerox machines.

"You, sir, have the right of counsel to defend yourself." Talking very slowly, "Do-you-understand-what-I'm-saying-to-you?"

Pretty offensive of him, but I said I understood and that Counselor Hirsh was to be my attorney, but looking across at tough, he-was-probably-a-major-in-the-Army Counselor Shallimar, and then at 4-F, because-of-no-arches Counselor Hirsh, I wasn't sure I had the right man. Lester asked for time alone with his client, inasmuch as I had until then been incarcerated.

"Objection! Held for observation," Shallimar corrected, jockeying for position early.

The judge said I could certainly have time with my attorney, and very slowly, was-that-all-right-with-me? It-was-all-right-with-me.

Lester, Judy and I went off to a small room where Lester briefed me. The hearing would be run like a regular trial, and presumably I knew the ground rules since I had seen trials on television and in the movies. I didn't want to admit that once when I was in bed with the flu I had become emotionally involved in the day-to-day proceedings of Divorce Court on television. But I did tell him that I knew all about the procedure having been on jury duty on a case where a woman sued an airline over the loss of her luggage. That didn't reassure him.

"We have problems. Usually your defense in a situation like this is to prove the defendant is capable of taking care of himself, that he knows the difference between right and wrong."

"Right and wrong. That's pretty deep."

"Uh, could you not make jokes? Crazy people joke their way to the gallows."

"What kind of gallows humor is that?"

"Uh, could you not make jokes?"

"Listen to Lester, honey."

"But how seriously can I take this? A hearing on my sanity."

"Could you try taking it seriously?"

"Who is this guy Shallimar anyway and what does he want?"

"He thinks he's a crusader and what he wants—is you committed."

"Let's put in a counterclaim and commit *him*."

"Could you let me be the lawyer? Now the way I figure his strategy . . . he's going to try to prove that you really think you saw God."

"I *did* see God."

"Right," said Lester, popping a little pill in his mouth. "That's what I figured."

"Wait a minute, Lester," Judy said. "That's all he's going to do?"

118

"Right."

"But everybody knows he said he saw God."

"Right."

"He's on record."

"Right."

Cutting through like Perry Mason, I said, "Then my *defense* will actually be their *prosecution*."

"Right." Popping another pill.

It was Catch-24.

"Of course, the judge could believe your story, but I wouldn't count on it. So all Shallimar has to do is prove it *is* your story. And who would tell such a story? An insane person, of course."

"That simply isn't fair," Judy said.

"Well, we have our day in court. We are being given the chance to prove our case."

"I think we should delay," I said. "Really build up an airtight case."

"Except you're in custody. The longer we delay, the longer they hold you."

"In Bellevue?"

"Listen, did they feed you? Legally, they've got to feed you."

"Who cares about that? Lester, get me off."

"We'll try. But as your lawyer, my legal advice to you is—to pray."

We then got down to figuring what evidence we could mount in my behalf, what witnesses we might be able to call in. The problem was so few people of stature had ever come out in active support of me. Lester, who had been trying to reach people all night, went off to place calls to a few more possibles, people who seemed to support me along the way, but as soon as it became clear to anyone that this was a sanity hearing, he politely declined. We had the kids on *The Good Earth,* but even they had never come right out and said they believed me, only that they felt I had a right to air my story. More important, Lester felt because they were the younger generation they might prejudice the judge against me.

Lester made his calls—no luck.

"What kind of guy is this judge?"

"Strict constructionist. He runs a tight court."

"He's Jewish, isn't he?" Judy asked. "Wouldn't that help?"

"Lavyne? He votes Republican. And his being Jewish could hurt, if the story offends him."

"This is a court of law!" I pronounced. "His personal feelings shouldn't come into it."

"My friend, *all* that counts are his personal feelings."

"I'm very depressed," Judy said.

"Yes, we all should be. Elaine was crying this morning."

"Isn't that pre-judging the case?"

"Lester, what can we do?" Judy asked.

"We're going to go in there and give them hell!"

"Yes, Lester, but how?" I said.

"We'll play it by ear!"

Lester then rose, gathered up his papers and said to me with conviction, "And if we lose, we can always appeal."

It looked like my lawyer was taking the strong legal position of hoping for a miracle.

The proceedings began with Shallimar making an opening statement in which he apologized. He would not have filed this complaint if not for the clear and present danger to others that I represented.

"We have all seen the strange, ill-dressed woman mumbling to herself on streetcorners and buses . . ." Come off it, Owen D. You've never been on a bus in your life. "But that type of mental illness, however sad, is harmless and I would never presume to bring charges against such a distressed soul. This man, however, has dangerous hallucinations . . ."

"Objection!" Lester called out.

"Counselor Shallimar, we will be dealing only in facts. Documentation, please."

That's good I thought. Only facts. The judge is being fair. Then it occurred to me. Facts. The facts could put me away! I was suddenly getting an upset stomach.

"The facts are that only a diabolically perverted man would . . ."

"Objection!"

"No, go on Counselor, develop your point."

"Only a sick, demented, dangerous man"—with what was going on in my stomach, he was right about the *sick*—"would publicly play upon the reverence and heartfelt devotion of people to the Lord God, Father of the Heavens . . ."

Yes, yes, who brought us forth bread from the earth.

Lester then had the chance to make his statement.

"Through the course of literary history, valuable creative people have examined their relationship with God. Dostoyevski, Sholom Aleichem—"—A little ethnic cuteness there—"Camus."

Camus? Lester, he came up empty-handed on God.

"And now this man, devoted husband, hardworking playwright, a veteran of the Armed Services," Lester? Six months in the Reserves? "has done the same as others before him. Whether we believe his story or not is totally irrelevant." My guy. He was going right at it.

"Objection! His Honor will determine relevance."

"That is true," the judge said.

"What is relevant is his right to make his contentions," Lester answered.

With a faint smile on his face Shallimar said, "Objection! Those rights are protected under The Bill of Rights. We are not here to determine those rights." I even knew that.

"I know what we're here to determine," the judge said. "Go on Counselor."

"Lester continued, "If this man claims he has met with God, that in itself is not a proof of his incompetence, only proof of his concern with the fundamentals of life, an outgrowth of his creative, searching spirit, his right as a literary figure to express himself in the style of

122

the great"—Lester paused to look at some notes he had made— "the great Judaeo-Christian New York Jewish Literary Establishment."

It sounded pretty thin to me. From what I could see, Lester was trying to get me off by claiming what didn't seem to be the most airtight legal point in the world— poetic license.

I then asked the judge if I could be excused for a moment due to terrible stomach. He called a ten-minute recess and a cop led me to a john and came inside the room with me. I thought he was going to follow me right into the bowl, but he stopped outside the stall. On the seat, a modern-day Luther, I called for my Lord to assist me.

"I know it's a lot to ask," I mumbled softly, knowing if the cop heard me, the next thing they'd be using that against me, "and I'm kind of embarrassed to be asking in this particular place, but I don't think it's going too well. I mean, if they prove—oh, you know the law. I need your help and I wouldn't be asking . . ." then out of nervy desperation, I said, "but I only did this for you."

God was silent.

I was led back inside where Shallimar began to build his case, starting with the sworn testimony of the twin doctors. In their opinion I was mentally unstable and a proper subject for care in a state mental hospital. That figured.

There is that moment in all the trials in the movies

and on TV where the defendant leans over and says something meaningful to his lawyer, who makes a note of it. I leaned over and said to Lester, "These guys see so many nutballs, they're over-nutballed." It came out under cross-examination as:

"Doctor Browder, is it not true that in your line of work you see so many nutballs, you are over-nutballed?"

"What was that question?" the judge asked, but it didn't matter anyway because it was clear that the judge felt that the doctors were doctors, and if a doctor says . . .

Doctors! When I was younger, doctors, premed students, anything with a potential doctor in it always got the girl. How the Jewish princesses loved their Jewish princes. A biology major had more prestige than me. Now doctors were back to haunt me. The Return of the Doctors.

"Doctors can hurt you in a deal like this," Lester said. "We need our own doctor. Have you got a friend who's a doctor?"

"All I have is a dentist."

"Doesn't Judy go to an analyst?"

"Yes."

"How about her?"

"She thinks I'm crazy."

Lester made a few notes on his legal pad, then said, "We'll come up with a good medical authority for the appeal."

"What about *now?*"

"There's not much we can do in the time. Anyway, this will all be over today."

"It will?"

"Oh, sure. Levine likes to get you in and out. He used to be a traffic judge. 'Traffic Judge Levine' they call him. We'll know tonight."

"We haven't had much of a shot." You fall into saying *"we"* when it's really *you* because it's easier to think it's not.

"We haven't. It's a lousy system. These competency and sanity procedures are the worst. Very little civil rights for the defendants."

"That's very informative, Lester."

"No, there's not much we can do about it. We could run in the ACLU as a protest, but it would be ruled irrelevant."

"They're going to send me up the river!"

"Or out on the island. But it will only be temporary, until the appeal, and we'll have more time to prepare for that. Meantime, you'll be all right. We'll visit. They'll keep you comfortable. And Mattewan has color television."

He thought I was crazy, too. My friend. My lawyer. Nobody believed me. There's nothing like being persecuted for a person who is being persecuted to feel persecuted. I looked back at Judy, remembering something Lester said once that divorces were such a drag that among lawyers the joke is—it's easier to just get your

125

mate committed—and was Judy trying to get rid of me? I was a paranoia festival.

I realized later on that Lester was doing the best he could under the circumstances. If he seemed matter-of-fact about the possible outcome, he was just taking a practical view so that if they *did* put me away momentarily, it wouldn't make me so crazy they'd have to *really* put me away—a logic you can only take so far, if you are *already* away.

Shallimar called his other witnesses, the arresting officers, who recounted the circumstances of the arrest, the J. P. Kearnsworth minister person who had been publicly criticizing me and who wasn't exactly a fan, who kept saying on the stand that I was dangerous, and a little bitty who turned out to be the cousin of the "God lives on NBC!" lady, testifying that her cousin had been placed in a rest home because of me. In cross-examination, Lester couldn't do much to budge the doctors—who could?—but he extracted that the Messrs. Kearney and Sabatello had used force on me during the arrest and don't people sometimes lose their tempers in a fight and might that not account for my behavior? They agreed it might, provided I wasn't psycho to start.

"Why don't we let His Honor decide that?" Lester said, rather pleased with himself.

He scored pretty well against Kearnsworth, too, I thought, getting him to admit he had declared himself to be a critic of mine long before these proceedings and since he had once called me "a vileness, a lowly liar and a clown," might possibly then be prejudiced.

"Fairly sloppy of old Owen D.," I said.

"I'm not so sure. All those times he said *dangerous*—that could build up subliminally."

You get so vulnerable in that kind of spot, you'll shift your opinion instantly. "Right. Tricky of that devil, wasn't it?"

The little lady cracked completely under cross-examination, admitting that her cousin was not really in a rest home under treatment, but on a dairy farm eating ice cream.

"Terrific, Lester. You have obliterated their case."

"Hardly. We don't really have anyone to call for the defense. I wouldn't put you up there. He'd take you apart."

"That's insulting."

"All he has to do is ask, 'Did you say this? Did you say that?' And you're finished."

"So who have we got?"

"Trust in the Lord."

Lester then stepped forward and he was beautiful. I think the way movie and TV lawyers act has influenced the way real-life lawyers now act, because he looked like he was on camera, our Lester, as he said with considerable panache, "The defense will call only one witness." And then with a flourish of his hand, "We call The Lord God."

127

Fantastic. I mean just fantastic. There is that expression, "his jaw dropped." Well, jaws really did drop. Everybody in the room—the judge, Shallimar, his witnesses, Judy, me—the room was filled with the dropping of jaws.

And then Lester just folded his arms and stood there, waiting—and the way he stood, waiting, made everybody else wait—even the judge, who finally said, "What is the meaning of this?"

"Your Honor, I have called on The Lord to take the stand."

"Are you trying to make a joke out of my courtroom?"

"No, your Honor."

And then Lester was wonderful. He said, "Your Honor, when I just asked The Lord to take the stand, in that fleeting moment after I called Him, was there not some trace of expectation in your mind? Could it—? What if—? Just a trace, your Honor. A flash. Wasn't there a hesitation in this room? Didn't you feel it? Didn't we all feel it? It was the possibility that God exists and if He exists, He could materialize to inhabit that chair—and who are we mortal men to doubt that possibility? In that moment, in that fleeting instant, when you, your Honor, when all of us in this room *didn't know*—in that heartbeat lies the doubt, the reasonable doubt that the defendant's story could be true. And as you withdraw to your chambers, please think back on that moment, that hesitation that contains reasonable doubt, and in your soul find for the defendant. The defense rests."

My buddy! I didn't know what good it would do, but he gave it a good shot. The pity is, as things turned out, we'll never know if Lester could have gotten me off with it.

The judge withdrew to consider the evidence and we remained in the courtroom and waited. Lester and Judy went out into the hall to stretch their legs. I was under guard.

Now the suddenness of what followed is very hard to describe and I'm going to be awfully longwinded in trying to give the feeling of it, but the closest thing to it in my experience was many years ago when I was listening to a World Series ball game on the radio between the Yankees and the Dodgers. It was the last of the ninth of a 0–0 ball game, Red Barber, the Dodger announcer, was announcing and Tommy Henrich was batting against Don Newcombe. The tension was tremendous. Then Red Barber said, "High drive. Home run. Ball game's over." Sudden as that. He didn't yell. He didn't give it a Mel Allen hoot. He just said it, understated, quickly. "Ball game's over." I resented it at the time, being a Yankee fan, feeling cheated out of hearing the announcer yelling. But Red Barber was right. Sudden things happen suddenly. And that's my buildup.

Lester came running in from the hall brandishing a newspaper. He got the judge to reopen for new evidence. The cavalry had arrived. The Georgetown University group had just released the results of their inquiry. They found, as they put it, "strong evidence to support the claims of a miracle." On the spot, the judge threw out the case against me. High drive. Home run. Ball game's over. I was a free man.

13

Ah, to be front page, prime time and sane again. Certified sane with a certified miracle. If you're in that situation what happens next is that the phone never stops ringing, people who interviewed you before try to use their deep friendship with you to interview you again, you become the center of a worldwide frenzy within the Religious Establishment, as leaders of all faiths don't quite know what to do with your miracle, whether to embrace you or worship you or ignore you, deciding finally to discuss you in an international interdenominational conference in a city unnamed because no one can agree on where to meet, several other universities form committees to report on the report from Georgetown under pressure from unhappy boards of trustees aggrieved that their universities had been scooped, a Presidential fact-finding board is formed of prominent clergymen which you decline to cooperate with, having done that sort of thing already, and which turns out to have been requested by none other than The Federal Bureau of Investigation who uncovered the fact that you had once participated in several Peace demonstrations and who wanted to make sure you were not a Commie plot, a stream of passersby becomes a constant in front of your apartment and the crowds would be even larger if not for the *New York Post* incorrectly listing your address in a story and sending scores of gawkers to the apartment of a poor photographer three blocks away who finds himself constantly being photographed by tourists, you are included on the route of the New York City sightseeing buses, fitting you in after Chinatown and before the U.N. and when your windows are open you can hear the bus P.A. system, "Yes, ladies and gentlemen, it is said God was recently in the basement of that house and the owner of that house . . ." Not owner, Mister. We only rent ". . . saw and spoke to God, as confirmed by experts at Georgetown University, which you may visit on your tour

132

of Washington and for which we provide you with discount exchange tickets—that very house, ladies and gentlemen. You may take pictures." And you speculate that once you're included in one of those things, you stay on forever. "Yes, ladies and gentlemen, it is said God was once in the basement of that house and the late owner of that house, God rest his soul . . ." "Yes, ladies and gentlemen on the site of that building once stood a building where it is said . . ." You also get to have a round man with a shaved head wearing a white robe stand in front of your apartment every day carrying a sign, although sign is an insufficient description because this thing had about ten pages of hand-lettered material tacked to a long pole and the best I could make out from it—I read a few lines each time I passed by— was that it contained his theory of God and the Universe, involving some interplanetary domino theory and the planet Earth is the southeast Asia of the heavens— don't ask. And an agent from an organization called Creative Management Associates calls to sell you on the idea of doing a one-hour network television special, which he will guarantee to be sold to a sponsor of taste like Hallmark Greeting Cards.

"One hour. Prime time."

"I don't think so."

"Your own production company. You take the profits."

"No, I don't think that's what I should be doing."

"You just get out there and rap."

"That would make for a pretty dull show, wouldn't it?"

"We build you up. Production values. A boys' choir."

"Sorry."

"A girls' choir?"

"Sorry."

"Billy Graham does TV. Oral Roberts. You can be better. You got a nice demography."

"A what?"

"New York. Jewish. We can get the big city markets."

And you vow to get your phone disconnected. But biggest of all of what happens to you in this situation which has created a commotion on your block and a crisis in Religion is that you make the cover of *Time* magazine. Right. All the marbles. Not a story about God. Not a wrap-up piece on the whole controversy. It was me, my face, a *Time* cover. There I was, rendered in color in a mystical setting, and in the background, various representations of God as Man has imagined Him through the ages. I was very impressed.

The day after the hearing, a couple of *Time* reporters had come to the house, but we didn't know it was for a cover story. They asked about my reactions to recent events, most particularly how did I feel about the sanity hearing and The Georgetown Report and I said something as profound as "Faith can move mountains." They printed that illuminating remark as well as their observation that "he is almost offhanded in his devotion, as though his belief is so clear to him, he is bored with the non-believing of others." What the reporter was picking up were the mechanical responses of an over-interviewed person. It was like Judy and I, the young couple at home, had no real personalities in front of people any longer, only a fabricated interview personality. We decided it was something to watch out for and we should try to act more ourselves. So we started to work out some dialogue that would make us seem more natural the next time someone came to the house.

"I'll answer the door and I'll say, 'Hi, nice to know you. This is my wife, Judy.' "

"And I'll say, 'Would you like some coffee?' "

"Or tea."

"Right. 'Would you like some coffee or tea? Or a drink?' "

"Good. We'll ask them if they want a drink, too. Let's run over that. 'Hi, nice to know you. This is my wife, Judy!' "

" 'Would you like some coffee or tea or a drink?' "

And then we caught ourselves and were very embarrassed at how over-involved we had become.

The cover story about me in typical *Time* fashion started with the news of the Georgetown findings, some background on the entire God situation, and then drifted all the way back to my childhood. They had extracted some pictures from my mother and there I was in *Time* magazine at age ten. The caption under the picture was a quote about me from a former elementary schoolteacher. It said, "No particular distinction." The next picture showed me at my Bar Mitzvah with a quote from the tutor who was run in at the last minute to help me remember my lines. The caption was, "Fairly slow." Then there was a picture of me taken a few years ago for a *Ladies' Home Journal* piece I did, just about when I first started selling articles and the caption was, "The yeast rises." And finally two pictures side by side, one of me going into Bellevue under arrest and the other, coming out of the courtroom exonerated and the captions were "Pre-miracle." "Post-miracle."

They had a quote from Owen D., who said, "Legal rulings notwithstanding, the man is a dangerous lunatic. If he wishes to go to court to sue for that, I would welcome the opportunity." Old soldiers never quit.

Cynthia   I-only-sleep-with-men-I'll-never-see-again Fox, a girl with whom I had a neurotic three-month relationship, and who distinguished herself afterward by baring her breasts at a Woman's Lib rally, a liberated action she never approximated with me, was quoted as *a former mistress*—hah!—who recalls me as "A drip." Don't you think that's a '40s word for a '70s girl?

And David Merrick, with whom I have absolutely no relationship, save the time I sat next to him once at a movie screening and frankly didn't know what to do with him being there—do you say, "Excuse me, Mr. Merrick, so long as I'm sitting next to you, I have these plays . . . ?" David Merrick was brought in to give the *Time* readers some idea of where my professional play-

136

wrighting career stood at the moment and was quoted as saying, "I haven't read anything of his personally, but his name is hot." This brought up a tricky moral point. Do you use your publicity—publicity about God at that—as a means of helping you sell your unsold plays? My moral decision was—you do. I called my agent immediately after the article appeared to say, "I'm hot. Do something." So she did. She sent the plays to David Merrick and he turned them down.

A person named Carlton Greener optioned both of them, though, and to bring it up to date on that aspect of my career, absolutely nothing has happened on productions for either. Greener says he's still working on raising money and it would be going better if the plays were on a religious theme, but since one is about a college kid who dumps a basketball game and the other is about a piano player, he says there is a rather tenuous association with the subject matter with which most people associate me, and it might help if I considered a rewrite, hopefully working God into them, or at least a heavenly spirit.

For all the press coverage, it was hard to tell where the public really stood on the miracle. Man in the street interviews and public opinion polls were turning up a lot of "Don't Know's," people apparently holding back for some official word from the Religious Establishment, which still hadn't been able to get itself together.

As for God Himself, He just hadn't been around lately. He had been giving me what I thought to be special attention. And then during the whole time of my arrest, detention and near-incarceration—nothing. I was speculating about this one afternoon. Judy was out shopping and the telephone man came to disconnect and remove the phone, only it wasn't the telephone man wearing those overalls and carrying a tool kit, it was Him.

"Hello, big shot," He said.

"It's you! Where have you been?"

"Listen, Mister Sanity Hearing, is that your business?"

"Do you know they almost put me away?"

"I know. He prays to me in the men's room yet."

"I needed your help."

"So things worked out anyway."

"They sure did. Did you see *Time* magazine?"

"I saw. So what kind of monkey business is that?"

"I thought it was impressive."

"I have an old saying. When the press agent becomes the news and not the client, it's time to fire the press agent."

Fire the press agent? Was that some euphemism for *doing me in?*

"And if I drop you, what do you do from here—go on to another God?"

I saw He really didn't mean to do me in. On the other hand, I hadn't thought of myself as a press agent in this.

"I really considered myself more a reporter," I said.

"With some pretty fancy bylines lately."

138

"I'm not looking for it. They even offered me a TV special and I turned it down."

"They offered him his own special."

"I said no."

"You know, I'm beginning to worry about all this publicity you're getting for yourself, personal. They could make *you* God, and I'd be out on the street."

"That couldn't happen."

"You wouldn't like to be God?"

"Of course not. I couldn't."

"You wouldn't want it anyway. It's a lot of heartburn."

What must it be like to be God? His face seemed to look kind of strained that day, like it *was* a lot of heartburn.

"So you'll do me a favor and keep it in line. I don't want on my hands a Pygmalion Monster."

I'm sure He meant either a "Pygmalion" or a "Frankenstein Monster" but I wasn't about to correct Him.

"I'll be careful about the interviews."

"Better there should be no more interviews."

"No more interviews?"

"No more TV either."

"No more TV?"

I was feeling shot down. He was right, though. I *had* been getting carried away with my own publicity.

"I'm sorry. You're right," I said.

"When love comes along, there is no right and wrong, your love is your love."

"Excuse me."

"Just something crossed my mind. From *West Side Story*. I saw it last night in a drive-in."

Some mad turn of phrase occurred to me and I was tempted to say, "Did you bring a date?" I'm sure He knew what I was thinking because He said,

"Watch it, my ipsy-pipsy. Don't take advantage."

"Well, what's the plan? What do I do now?" I asked.

"Let's stay with what we got. See how it develops."

"I shouldn't do anything?"

"What do you want, to help with God's word or be a cover boy?"

A little of both, I was thinking.

"You give a fella a little turn in the limelight, he wants to be a dancer."

No more TV! No more interviews!

"There are people who would be happier with less. Monks. They don't become stars, they grow vegetables."

"Of course I'll do as you wish."

"Good. Enough with the promotion and the exploitation. We gave the world the ball, let them run with it!"

He had some curious ways of expressing Himself.

"So that is what I wanted to say to you. Now I'll do the phone."

"You're going to do the phone?"

"What do you think? I wouldn't know how to do it?"

And He did it. He actually disconnected the phone

140

like a telephone man, working very efficiently, while I looked on, fascinated.

"God is boundless," He said.

Then He put the disconnected phone into his tool box, snapped the box shut, smiled as though He just thought of something clever to say—and said:

"Don't call us. We'll call you."

14

HAVING just been muzzled by The Lord, and having recently lived in—as the Chinese curse goes—"interesting
times," I decided Judy and I had earned a vacation. The
only thing that seemed to require my attention was the
big all-faith international conference which was being
called to discuss the miracle, and that was still far from
being worked out. Rome wanted it in Rome, the Eastern
religious leaders wanted it in the East, the West in the

West. It was like they were picking a site for the Olympic Games.

It was a good time to get away. But where do you go if you're a phasing-yourself-out *Time* cover story? I didn't want to go too far away from New York, feeling I should at least stay available to the press if some questions came up. But I didn't want to go where I would attract attention, having the arrogance to assume I would.

We decided to rent a house in the woods near Sag Harbor out on Long Island. Sag Harbor is largely a middle-class boating community, the poor sister in The Hamptons area. It doesn't have the chic of say, East Hampton. And if God didn't want me on television attracting attention, He certainly wouldn't have approved of me in East Hampton, a smug little town that prides itself on its number of show business stars, pretending to ignore them, while really staring at them. When I was away, nobody in Sag Harbor recognized me or cared, except for one girl whom I'll get to, but in East Hampton where I went to the movies twice, I was stopped twice, by one person who was sure I looked familiar because I was one of the Beatles, and another who thought I was Elliott Gould.

We rented a house for the month, and rented a car, and I got to wondering would I have needed this vacation which required me to take all this money out of personal savings, if I hadn't been under a strain from

143

my experience? Plus if you add up all the money I spent on printing and supplies, to say nothing of the salary I paid Judy—and it wasn't just bookkeeping, she had her own bank account—I was now out over $3,500 on the deal. The cost of seeing God has risen since Moses' day.

Well, it was vacation time for us, but you don't just take off for vacation in New York—leaving the city is an entire anti-burglary project. I took Judy's best jewelry to the vault; hooked up all the living-room lights with a timer to make it look like someone was home; pasted burglar-alarm stickers on the windows, even though we had no burglar alarm; had the post office hold the mail; packed our hi-fi system and television set into the car, since they were the most expensive appliances we owned and didn't want anyone stealing them—and wondered if I'd ever reach the point of being able to ask Him to keep an eye on the apartment when we were away.

A few days later, while lying on the beach, I turned to Judy and trying to be funny, but also meaning it, said, "Isn't it nice to be relaxing here, while back in the city we're being burglarized?"

"Don't worry, Hon. We have the man with the signs."

"He's probably our burglar."

"He'll keep an eye on things."

"I'll bet."

"He said he would."

"You talked to him?"

"He's very nice."

144

"He's a religious fanatic, or some kind of fanatic."

"Now, dear, some people would call you the same."

"Well, I'm sure he knows we're away. He saw us going."

"Honey, relax, I told him we'd be away a month—and to make sure everything would be all right, I gave him a key."

"What? You gave that nut a key to our house?"

"You have to have faith in people, Darling. He's very smart and gentle. Did you ever read his signs?"

"You gave him a key? What's the matter with you? Why did you give him a key?"

"So he can water the plants."

Of course, nothing went wrong in the apartment. We were to return home to find the parade of sightseers had diminished somewhat, but was still going on, oblivious of the fact that we left and oblivious of the fact that we were back. It had a life of its own without us. And the man with the signs was still there. He had watered the plants.

It was out on Long Island where we had the only trouble.

Is God in East Hampton? said the headline of the *East Hampton Star,* going on to report that someone thought they had spotted me in town, and did that mean that God was summering in East Hampton? It sounded tongue in cheek, but you couldn't tell. You see, they're so proud of *who* summers out there, God would have been a real coup.

It made me cautious about appearing too openly in public. I really didn't want a lot of scenes on our vacation, and sure enough, some hysteric insisted she saw God sitting in a local potato field and that was good for a story the following week. Then it all died down. I stayed close to the house except when we went to the beach, and luckily, we found a fairly secluded beach where we'd go each day. We even stopped buying newspapers and I tried to get God off my mind for a while. I figured if anything really urgent came up that He wanted to tell me, He could just show up or float me a note in a bottle or something.

Judy decided she had been getting too much sun, so on this particular afternoon she stayed back at the house. I went to the beach alone, setting myself up a couple of hundred yards away from the handful of people who were there. As the day went on, they gradually left and I was sitting there alone. Then I noticed this absolutely beautiful suntanned girl walking along in a bikini—long legs, small waist, lovely breasts—an incredible figure. She had to be one of the best-looking girls I ever saw in my life. She looked at me, then walked right toward me. She stopped in front of me and was staring.

"It's you," she said.

"It is?"

"The Miracle Claimant." It really sounded odd hearing it in speech like that.

"I think you're mistaken. I'm Elliott Gould."

146

"No, I'd know you. It's you. My God, it's you!"

"You're really mistaken—"

"I was just walking along—and it's *you!*"

"You have me confused—"

"God's will has brought me to this crossroads."

"I don't think He gets involved in beaches."

"It is a sign from Heaven."

"You're exaggerating, Miss."

"On this beach. You. I."

"Now, Miss—"

"What was I before this?"

"Excuse me but I was reading—"

"I was a piece of driftwood on life's shore. Thank you, Lord, for sending him to me."

"I was just sitting here—"

"His ways are strange. But it is ordained. So be it."

"So be what?"

"In a summer of searching, comes this spiritual happiness."

Then she dropped to her knees, looked into my eyes and said, "My love, my heavenly love. Fuck me."

"Huh?"

"Fuck me. Enter me with your holy presence."

"Now, look—"

"Sanctify my womb."

"Lady!"

"Give meaning to my life with your golden staff."

Then this gorgeous thing started to remove her bikini, murmuring, "It's a sign, a sign." She was now completely naked, kneeling in front of me with that body of hers saying,

"Love me, my heavenly love. Squirm with me until the heavenly juices flow."

I was in some spot.

She leaned forward, as I sat frozen in my beach chair, and put her arms around me.

"I'm warm and moist for you. Feel how warm. Oh, my God, fuck me, fuck me, fuck me."

Nervously I put my hands up to push her away and found her breasts in them.

"Uplift me. Purify me!" She looked pretty clean to me.

Catching myself—"Now listen here. I'm a married man."

"There is no one to see us." Which was true enough.

"Only God, who Himself ordained this." I think that was stretching it a bit.

"It's a miracle. A miracle."

"It's not a miracle."

"It is."

"It's a chance happenstance."

"It's a miracle. Enter me. Enter me with your holy presence."

"You are very mistaken."

"Enter me with your holy presence!"

"Look, I am not holy. I'm no part of God. He's just an acquaintance."

And I got up, my erection and moral upbringing

showing, gathered up my chair and towel and started to leave. After all, I don't mind selling my unsold plays off of knowing God, but using it to commit an act of adultery with a crazy chick on a public beach . . .

She followed along the sands, clinging to me.

"Let the heavens rejoice for our song of love."

"Yes, yes, wonderful."

I started walking, then running, this naked creature groveling after me. I was flopping across the beach, my feet halfway out of my sneakers, the beach chair banging against my leg, running away from one of the best package deals of the summer tourist season.

"Do not reject God's will!"

If that was God's will, Job was never so lucky. We had now reached the path through the dunes where the cars were parked. There were some stragglers packing up to leave and they saw us bursting over the crest of the dunes, this naked girl clutching at me, and me with my beach chair, huffing and puffing—a scene out of a perverse porno movie. We were *Tessie and the Geriatric.*

"Animals!" a woman screamed, scooping up her two children. An older couple looked on, furious at this ultimate insult from "the summer people."

The girl stopped. "My love, my holy love," she called out. Then she slowly ran her fingers across her naked body and arched her middle toward me.

"I'll be waiting—waiting for your golden staff through eternity. 324–6179. Sonya."

149

It all happened fast as a sudden shower and that is what I needed when I got back. Judy asked me why I seemed so nervous, but I said it was nothing. I just couldn't bring myself to tell her and never did until now, and I know this is kind of a cheap way to tell you, Honey, but look at it this way. The same guilt and sexual inhibitions that prevented me from saying anything to you, also prevented me from doing it with her—so I'd say it's a tie ball game.

But can you imagine a beautiful girl like that groveling after me? It was better than being a doctor.

15

ALTHOUGH we weren't reading newspapers every day
while we were away, we would catch a glance now and
then—and there was one running story about the latest
developments on that international conference of religious leaders. At that point, three weeks after we left
New York, they were still confused, still picking a site
and nowhere on an agenda. Elsewhere, the pot having
boiled, it continued to simmer with reports of God-
sightings, which now regularly found their way into the
news as filler items. One thing I had done was put the

Virgin Mary sightings out of business for a while.

God was said to have: shown up in Sarasota, Florida, as an extra umpire in a Little League game; turned up in a laundry room of a Dallas housewife, and as the woman reported it, He gave her advice on the best laundry detergent to use; made a flamboyant appearance on the Israeli border where, according to an old Israeli farmer, "He shot an Arab guerrilla in the *tuchis.*"

He hadn't visited me in Sag Harbor, although I could have sworn I spotted Him down by the water drinking beer during the Whalers' Festival. Is it possible He enjoys doing little walk-ons like Alfred Hitchcock?

The month's vacation was coming to a close and we were going to wind up by eating some major meals at the house. I went into town to help Judy with the shopping and there in the Sag Harbor A & P, the vacation ended early.

The store, which sometimes sells paperback books in cardboard racks alongside the cookies, had set up an enormous paperback display. It was the first thing you saw when you came in. It was created for one book, featured one book, and that one book was *The Man Who Saw God.* It was my life's story. My life's story! I never told anybody my life's story. I didn't even know it. And there was this unauthorized, pirate biography, my face on the cover, $1.25. I bought a copy. I paid my money for a copy of a book about me. It was written by somebody named F. X. Franckks, which sounded like a made-up name to me, and I just hoped for sentimental reasons that it wasn't written by some struggling playwright selling out for money. *The Man Who Saw God.* The gall! My life was *my* life. It wasn't public domain. Actually, when we got home and read it, we saw it wasn't even my life. Under a chapter, "Cleanliness Is Next to Godliness":

> In his childish innocence, he had heard the expression, "Cleanliness is next to Godliness." Thinking this was a way to be near his Lord, this sweet child bathed often, sometimes as often as three times a day. This delightful anecdote shows the emerging kinship he felt with God even at the tender age of thirteen. It was only when his father said, "My sweet son, it is only an expression." "An expression?" he answered. "Yes. A wish that people should be clean, but not to be taken literally." "Oh," he said. "I hope I have not offended God." Offended God! Little did he know that God sees all and God would remember!

I love that "delightful anecdote" for a couple of reasons. One, my parents were divorced when I was six and I haven't seen my father since. And two, we only had a shower, we never owned a bathtub.

From the chapter, "A Man of Prayer":

> . . . from the earliest he would say his prayers at night, always the same prayer, "God bless

Mommy and God bless Daddy, God bless everything that grows and the animals and the children of all nations." Could God resist such a charming tyke?

So open was he in his faith, so unashamed before his God, he was to repeat this prayer every night of his life before he went to bed, even when he had grown stronger and taller of limb, into his teens, into his twenties, even into his thirties. The child grown to a man, still saying his prayers at night, the same prayer, "God bless Mommy and God bless Daddy, God bless everything that grows and the animals and the children of all nations." Who among us can say the same for ourselves?

Who indeed! The book jumped back and forth from completely fabricated episodes to episodes fabricated from an occasional fact. The fact is, as was mentioned earlier, I had once sung in my high school chorus. The writer probably dug up a copy of the DeWitt Clinton High School Yearbook, and this information became— "A Young Rebel":

While other young men were venting their aggressions in sporting pursuits, he chose a more solemn path. He was to become the soloist with his high school chorus, lifting his voice on high in performances of great hymns in praise of God. Yes, God heard!

154

In high school, the closest I ever came to a solo was my big "Dry Bones" number and, ironically, God might have heard, because the whole solo consisted of me stepping in front of the stage and shouting, "Yeah, Lawd!"

I figured out what Mister, or could it have been Miss? F. X. Franckks's game was—or perhaps it was the notion of the publisher, Reverence Books. Reverence Books? I never heard of them and I'm sure it was formed for the sole purpose of publishing this thing. They figured if they told the story about me straight, people would think—is that all he is? What's so special about him? God could have talked to *me*. And they'd start resenting the hero of the piece. Better to put me in a saintly category for people to look up to and think—he is such a pure, Godly person. Is it any wonder God chose him and not me? What a wonderful, inspirational story. They were going right after the people who like to read that kind of wonderful, inspirational story.

And they cleaned up any sex life I had. I mean I wasn't a Warren Beatty, but I certainly wasn't, as the book told it, "A Man Restrained."

> In a world of lowered morals, of adultery and pre-marital intercourse, of immorality in word and deed, in film and book, in song and story, he moved through this world, a man restrained. The temptations were many. Living in a city such as New York with its Greenwich Village, he was

155

easy prey for what has become known as The New Sex. It is a climate in which girls walk about freely without wearing foundation garments. So he carried in his wallet at all times for protection . . .

The lewd among us probably think that F.X. was about to say, "for protection . . . a rubber prophylactic." For shame, easy preys of The New Sex.

> . . . he carried in his wallet at all times for protection . . . a poem:
>> The sins of the flesh can break a man
>> Destroy his moral carriage,
>> But God prefers a Godly man
>> Who saves himself for marriage.
>>   Anon.

Judy he also cleaned up. Not to say my wife needed cleaning up, mind you. She was, before I met her, a terrific lady who held a job, had an apartment, had a social life, with no major skeletons in her closet. She was not, however, "The Heavenly Maiden."

> His Judith. They met at an interdenominational retreat.

We met at a noisy party.

> They courted by making rounds of religious services of all faiths. A religious person, her first words to him were, "My only desire is to keep a kosher home." In the Jewish faith, a kosher home

156

is orthodoxy, a maintaining of the Old Testament rituals, and these were the first words she spoke to him, to establish between them a rich God-bound relationship.

Her first words to me as I recall, after we had danced to an entire Aretha Franklin album without speaking were, "I just want to get something straight about tonight. I'm not going to bed with you."

He then went on to my encounters with God, which were told pretty much as I had reported them, Reverence Books operating on the assumption no doubt that this part of the story was too well publicized to embellish too much.

And then a concluding chapter, "The Man Who Saw God Looks to the Future," which was the most extraordinary of all because it quoted me at great length saying inspirational things like, "We must all pull ourselves up by our religious bootstraps."

And what of me? Well, that's what the book said:

> What of him? What is there left for a man who has seen God? We ask too often in our competitive world for a man to prove himself over and over again, as though one great noble deed has no virtue. It is clear that he need do no more than he has done to earn our respect. For he passed among us . . .

It sounded like I was dead.

. . . and he touched the heavens. This then is
his story. Let it stand as thus, without further
exploitation of him. This then is his book. Let
it stand as definitive without further books at-
tempting to make profit from or be disrespectful
of—The Man Who Has Seen God.

Pretty clever. In one nice sweep, our writer tells our
readers that the story is over and the public never has to
buy another book on the subject now that they have his.
That's taking care of the competition.

After our initial anger in seeing the book, as we
started to read it, Judy and I began to warm to it. It was
really quite funny to us, all that fantastic nonsense, and
we spent the night reading sections to each other and
cracking up.

"But what should we do about it?" I said.

"We could sue."

"That would only make more news."

"It still might discredit it," Judy said.

"On the other hand, it does make me out to be a very
nice person."

"Sure. Merely a saint."

Then we started repeating lines and laughing all over
again until we finally fell asleep.

God didn't think it was so funny.

He woke me up that night, motioning me to follow
Him upstairs to the living room. I left Judy sleeping and
tiptoed behind Him. He was wearing gray-striped

pants, a white shirt with garters holding up the sleeves, a bow tie and a green eyeshade. He looked like a Las Vegas blackjack dealer. It turned out it was His idea of what a book editor looks like.

"What do you call this?" He said, brandishing a copy of the book.

"Yes, we had a good laugh over it."

"Hah, hah. This is black humor?"

"Well, it's so fantastic—"

"You don't come off so bad, though. The pussycat of history. Next to you Saint Francis of Assisi was the Mafia."

"It's their marketing strategy. They're doing that to sell books."

"You're telling me about marketing? I got the number-one best seller."

"I think it's just something we can laugh off—"

"Listen to this." He started to read a section He had circled with a grease pencil. " 'Thank you, Lord, for choosing me of all men. Thank *you*, the Lord said, for living a life so pure in heart and innocent in spirit.' "

"Well, that's a certain liberty—"

"In nineteen forty-four when you stole a toy bone from the five-and-ten for your dog—was pure in heart and innocent in spirit?"

"Nineteen forty-four?"

"In nineteen-fifty when you felt up Barbara Gott-schmidt in her living room with her mother and father sleeping in the bedroom and she said, 'Please don't' and you did anyway—was pure in heart and innocent in spirit?"

"Right, there was a Barbara Gottschmidt—"

"In nineteen sixty-one when you took off on your income tax thirty dollars for sales tax for cigarettes when you had already stopped smoking—was pure in heart and innocent in spirit?"

"It was a clerical error."

"In the years nineteen sixty-three to nineteen sixty-eight when you were a bachelor in New York and you did such dirty things with ladies I wouldn't even want to repeat such *shmutz*—was pure in heart and innocent in spirit? What do you say to that? I don't see any of that in the book."

My life flashed before me. It was Judgment Day. This is the way it happened. God comes to your bed, wakes you up and reads you your life.

He continued from the book. " 'Even as a teenager, he felt honesty is the best policy.' So tell me which person in this room cheated on his Spanish Regents Exam?"

"I couldn't help seeing his paper!"

" 'Yes, he was fortunate beyond fortune to find God, but in a world of chicanery and deceit, was not the Lord lucky to find him?' So lucky I am, I can't stand it."

"I repent," I shouted. "I repent all my sins! Judgment Day! Judgment Day!"

"Oh, be quiet. You'll wake your wife."

"It's not Judgment Day?"

"First, it's night, it's not day. Second, I don't do judgments. This is editing we're doing."

"It is?"

"The whole world needs editing. But it's the book I'm talking about. I circled the bad parts."

Nearly the entire book was circled.

"Please understand. This is an unauthorized biography."

"No fooling."

"And of course it's wildly inaccurate."

"And who is the star of the story and who is just a supporting character?"

"It's not quite the emphasis I would have given—"

"Who is suddenly a celebrity with a whole book about him and who is the forgotten party?"

"F. X. Franckks. Reverence Books. They're the ones who did it!"

" 'The Man Who Saw God.' Before me, you were, 'The Man Who Saw Chopped Liver.' "

"I know and I'm eternally grateful."

"Don't give me eternally. You don't know from eternally. 'Pull ourselves up by our religious bootstraps.' That's the dumbest thing I ever heard."

"I never said it!"

"Tell me you don't like the idea of a book about you?"

"It's so ludicrous—"

"Tell me you don't like the idea of being in the public library in the "B" for Biography section with Sigmund Freud and Mickey Mantle?"

"Well, it's a paperback. That's not like a hardcover book."

"They're putting it out hardcover—also leatherbound for the very devout."

"They are?"

"So what do you plan to do about it?"

"Maybe the thing to do is just ignore it, and let it die out on its own."

"Ten thousand copies a week it's selling!"

"Really?"

"Outselling the Bible in some places."

"I'm sorry."

"Not that the Bible is such a bargain—talk about inaccurate. But I think if you want to make me feel better, you'll disown this book."

"I do. I disown it very much."

"Not to me. To the public."

"But I shouldn't get into public statements. I've been phasing myself out like you said."

"This is phasing out? This is bigger than *Time*. I turn my back. I go away on a little vacation—"

"*You* go on vacation? Where? How?"

"It's very complicated. You wouldn't understand. Anyway, I come back and see this."

"Listen, were you at the Whalers' Festival?"

"Don't change the subject. Do something please about this."

"What?"

"That's up to you. I'm just an editor."

"I'll see what I can do."

"If it's not too much trouble. As I see from this book, you're a pretty important fella. 'Yeah, Lawd!' "

And He tipped His green eyeshade and left.

I stayed up the rest of the night worrying. When Judy woke up, I told her that God had been there.

"Here? In Sag Harbor?"

"That's right."

"Well, for heaven's sake, don't tell anybody. You'll kill the area."

"This is serious. He's unhappy about the book."

"Then why did He let it get published?"

"He doesn't make those decisions. He's an editor not a censor."

"I see," she said, uncertainly.

I decided to make a brief, unemotional statement to the press. I said the book was a work of pure fiction and I did not endorse it. I phoned this into *The New York Times* and it was absolutely the wrong decision because my statement made news, gave a giant publicity boost to the book, and sales shot up even higher. Reverence Books in their next printing even used my quote as a cover blurb with a headline: SEE FOR YOURSELF—FACT OR FICTION?

163

On the day before we went back to New York, I went down to the ocean for a last swim. I had said that if God wanted me while I was away He could just show up or float me a note in a bottle. He had already shown up. This time He floated me a note. It said:

```
Boy, oh boy, is someone in trouble with
someone, only I don't want to mention
names.
```

It got worse. We returned to New York to observe *The Man Who Saw God* rise to the top of the hardcover and paperback best-seller lists simultaneously. And the publishing industry being what it is, there were soon several unauthorized spin-offs of the unauthorized original.

There was *Miracle Claimant*—a poorly written fantasy of a fantasy. "He walked through life hearing an inner voice . . ." It made me sound like a schizo.

Dios y Hombre—A Spanish language quickie selling for a quarter in vending machines.

The True Adventures of the Man Who Saw God—a comic-book version of the whole deal.

And *God's Friend*—a really sticky version that practically made it into a homosexual relationship.

The one that floored me though was *The Man Who Saw God's Picture Album*—which was actually an album of original pictures of me at various stages of my life, generously supplied the publisher by my mother.

"Mother, those people are exploiters. How dare you give them that stuff?"

"They gave me two hundred dollars."

"But you don't need that money. And those pictures are private! That's terrible."

"Terrible? How about being the only not-Grandmother in the condominium? Is that terrible?"

"What does that have to do with it?"

"Everybody here has pictures of babies."

"So?"

"So now when they show from their children, babies —I can show from my son, a check. You work with what you got."

Meanwhile, the true and original F. X. Franckks's version was going great guns and in one of the wonderful promotion reversals, who was going to make an appearance on Johnny Carson, but F. X. Franckks himself.

F. X. Franckks turned out to be a he—a very slightly built, meek man with thin lips and a thin little voice. But what was most striking about him, considering he had stolen my life and then written a whole life that wasn't my life, was his absolute sincerity.

Johnny Carson asked him, "Why did you write this book?"

"A good question, Mr. Carson, a very good question. Why did I write this book? I wrote this book because this is a glorious story, one of the most glorious in the history of Man and God, and we should not be deprived of its glorious truth."

"Your subject has questioned its truth, hasn't he?"

"That is a good point, Mr. Carson, a very good point. Why has he questioned its truth? He has questioned its truth because, as a result of his experience, he is a man so touched by grace, he is not a satisfactory judge of his own life."

"And how did you get the information for the book?"

"How did I get the information for the book? I got the information for the book by talking to hundreds of people to piece together the jigsaw of a life. A clear picture emerged of a man destined by his goodness to be chosen by God."

Incredible. He actually believed what he had written. That's why his piracy was so much better than anybody else's. In his mind, it *was* the story of my life.

We met once. He was standing outside the house one afternoon, waiting for me.

"Sir?" he said.

"Yes?"

"Sir?"

"Yes?"

"I am . . ."

He paused. The moment obviously held great solemnity for him.

"I am . . . that is . . . my name is . . . F. . . . X. . . ." The pauses were unbearable.

"Franckks!" I blurted out.

"Yes . . . F. . . . X. . . . Franckks. And . . . and I am . . ."

166

"You are?" I was in a Pinter play.

"I am very . . . pleased . . . very honored . . ." John Gielgud couldn't have delivered it better. ". . . to meet . . . you."

"Well, Mr. Franckks—"

"And I just . . . wanted . . . to say . . . that . . ."

He couldn't make it. Overcome with emotion, he leaned forward and gave me a wet kiss on the cheek. Ick. This was a very strange person.

16

THE international all-faith conference to deal with the miracle was finally shaping up and since we live in an age of shorthand, it was to be called ALLFAITH. Representatives of every organized religion in the world were to attend and they finally settled on an off-the-beaten-path site—New York City, and borrowed a hall —The U.N.

I wasn't very enthused about having still another judgment made of my contentions, but I figured this one was inevitable. Many people throughout the world had been waiting for a response from high religious circles before committing themselves on the miracle. So by now, the Religious Establishment was under great pressure to take some kind of position.

I started making phonecalls to determine what role I would play in the conference, figuring a report to the delegates would be in order, or an address of welcome to the delegates, or a cocktail reception with the delegates. Very grandiose of me. I was told by the ALL-FAITH events chairman, whom I finally got to after talking to the delegates chairman, to whom I was transferred by the inquiry chairman, that they had no intention of having me present for the conference. They had all the information they needed—it was a matter of sorting it out on a factual and philosophic basis and my presence would only sully the objectivity of the conference.

It was the usual prejudice toward me of formal religious leaders. I was not yet, in their eyes, The Man Who Saw God, and during the conference I was actually to become referred to as "that person."

I rationalized that it was just as well for me to stay home, since my attendance there might seem to God to be some more headline-grabbing. As it was, there was no sign of Him again and I permitted myself the sacrilege of thinking He was merely sulking over the best-seller lists.

ALLFAITH was going to be big—bigger than I

would have liked, and more absolute, too. The Religious Establishment, slow to move at first, was now sweeping in with a flourish and taking center stage. *They* would give their verdict on the miracle. They were presuming to speak for everyone on the subject—and if you didn't happen to practice a formal religion, well, you were about to be spoken for.

The conference was to run seven days, presided over by a rotating committee of twenty-four chairmen, and underneath them, a delegates assembly broken down into operating units of assorted committees and sub-committees, in turn presided over by group leaders and coordinators, interspersed with multi-lingual transla-tors, and out of this bureaucrat's free-fall—they were going to issue The Word on The Word. The miracle didn't happen unless they said so.

Two thousand delegates began arriving from around the world, all "Top Brass Religiosos" as *Variety* put it. New York City went all out. "Welcome ALLFAITH" signs were up on windows of department stores, Horn & Hardarts, shoe stores, restaurants and the novelty stores around Times Square. Times Square itself was shaped up for the event, and under pressure from City Hall, bookstores that had been selling *Butch Trade, Sex Kit-ten, Whip Love* and other favorites, had stocked up on F. X. Franckks and Norman Vincent Peale. The grind movies that regularly showed such delicacies as *The Spy Who Came in from the Pussy* were now holding Bible Movie Festivals.

170

There was one awkward incident, though, involving Dirty Louie, a grizzly pornie entrepreneur who ran a nickelodeon, except you put quarters in, that featured continuous performances of the sex act in every possible position by every possible combination. Dirty Louie, a purist in his art, refused to be coerced by City Hall, and his one concession was to paint over the sign on his store which said, "Girls! Girls! Girls!" and substitute it with "Nuns! Nuns! Nuns!" Inside, Louie had pictures of his girls dressed as nuns in compromised positions. The thing is, he was doing a big business when they locked him up.

The conference had the effect of creating a religious renaissance in New York. Having all these religions assembled in one place was like having the World Series in town and you cheered for your favorite religion. Sales volume went way up on every kind of religious artifact. The people who sell umbrellas on the sidewalks were hawking beads, crosses and Stars of David. Cartier's had a special window of religious jewelry priced at over $3,000 and there was a line down the block to look at it, the kind of line that would usually attract the pretzel man, who showed up with his cart all right, but instead of pretzels, there were fifty-cent Jesus on the Cross-es and buttons that said "ALLFAITH."

There was to be round-the-clock television coverage by the non-commercial stations, constant spot reports and news specials on the major stations, and transmissions by worldwide satellite. It really was like having the

World Series in town. The conference even had its own scorecard, an ALLFAITH Souvenir Program, pictures of the players.

On the eve of the conference, Billy Graham jetted into New York to hold an open-air meeting in the Sheep Meadow in Central Park, which drew an estimated 150,000 people, while Glen Campbell filled Shea Stadium with "An Evening of Spiritual Singing."

Opening day arrived and among the greeters were President Nixon, the Governor, the Mayor, some members of the original cast of the U.N., and there was the New York Philharmonic Orchestra and the Mormon Tabernacle Choir doing Beethoven's Ninth, followed by benedictory prayers by each of the participating religions, which in a preview of things to come, lasted for four and a half hours.

Once under way, the first three days of the conference were dominated by a philosophic rivalry over which religion had the truest interpretation of God. There was a parade of speakers, day and night, each using his allotted time before the delegates to champion his particular denomination's point of view. It came across on television like a marathon sermonette.

Meanwhile, the real work—what would you call it, miracle analysis?—was going on behind closed doors, like the back room lobbying at a political convention. Commenting on this, a *New Yorker* cartoon appeared showing delegates seated as if at a nominating convention underneath political-style banners saying, "Hun-

garian Baptist," "Dutch Reformed," "Serbian Ortho-
dox." Across the street from the U.N., Paul Krassner,
Jerry Rubin and Abbie Hoffman of the original Yippies
established, for their own sense of satire, a "street
church" conducting services on the sidewalk consisting
of readings from their church's scriptures—the "scriptures" being news stories about the miracle as reported
by the press. Under complaints from delegates to the
conference, the "church" was dispersed, the Yippies
claiming immunity from arrest under an American Flag
and a Star of David.

By the fourth day, reports indicated that the conference was dividing into seven major factions. The bona
fide miracle group: a miracle *has* taken place. Let us
rejoice. The modified miracle group: a miracle *should
have* taken place. Let us rejoice. The qualified miracle
group: a miracle *may have* taken place. Let us embrace.
The verified miracle group: *has* a miracle taken place?
Let us discuss. The irrelevant miracle group: a miracle
is irrelevant. Let us go beyond. The potential miracle
group: a miracle *is soon* to take place. Let us plan. And
finally, the anti-miracle group: a miracle *has not* taken
place—with several subfactions within the faction. Let
us forget. Let us condone. Let us condemn. Let us
adjourn.

By the fifth day I was climbing the wall. They were
talking about me. I was "that person" and I wasn't even
there. F. X. Franckks was there, writing an article for
Life. Norman Mailer was there, writing a book on it.

173

Candice Bergen was there, sent by *Cosmopolitan* for "The Swinging Girl's View of The Big Guy."

"Judy, I have to go."

"You can't. You're not invited."

"But the conference is drifting. I can do something."

"Oh, you can? God isn't playing God. Why should you?"

She was right, of course, but I decided to crash the party anyway. I just had to see what was happening for myself. I couldn't walk right in, though, or I'd be recognized. My plan was to do it with a disguise. I went into a little import store in my neighborhood and outfitted myself. Wearing a Moroccan fez, a djellaba, sunglasses and a veil—I know a veil is for women, but who'd know what kind of religious cult I was into?—I entered the press gate as Aba Zeb of the *Rabat Herald*.

Once I got into the U.N. itself, I saw that there were security guards all over the place. If most of the delegates' work was being conducted behind closed doors, the doors were closed to me. I realized very quickly I was better off at home watching on television in a sweatshirt and dungarees than in the General Assembly in my djellaba and veil.

So long as I had gone to all that trouble, I decided to at least stay through the rest of the session. I found myself a seat in the press section next to a reporter from *The Times* whom I happened to know, and I crouched down so he wouldn't recognize me, but he wasn't the one to give me trouble. An Arab colleague approached

174

me and said something in our native tongue. I nodded knowingly and blessed him with my hand, making the sign of nuclear disarmament in the air. He must have thought I was a wierdo because he shook his head and walked away. Before I got out of there I was stopped several other times by delegates anxious to know my persuasion. I made my sign and moved on, leaving them to think they had just been blessed by a very religious person.

On the podium, the general position speeches of the first few days had given way to declamations by the various factions at the conference. At bat, was a fiery German Calvinist taking a strong anti-miracle, let-us-condemn position. This guy had a temper. The George-town group was ridiculed, I was ridiculed, the confer-ence was ridiculed, and finally, running out of targets, but still working under full steam, God was ridiculed for letting it all happen. Now that's angry.

Next was a Moslem who referred to this as a green time when ideas might flourish, but alas, as to miracles, this miracle was not written. I was listening intensely through my headphones to the puzzlement of the people around me wondering why in the world an Arab needed a translation from the Arabic.

Then came a little Catholic nun from France, a sin-cere young girl with a lovely voice. She pleaded with the delegates to stop bickering, to try to reach some level of understanding.

"The true miracle is that we are all here together,"

175

she said. "So let us seize this miracle and issue one re-sounding statement for peace in the world. Let us tell the rulers of all our nations to seize the moment with us. I move that we close this conference to further discussion of whether or not a miracle has taken place, and that we discuss the specific ways that we can effect social change, that we try together for a new miracle on earth by people of all nations of all faiths, working for a true brotherhood and gentleness before God."

I was very touched by her speech, but I'm afraid the delegation was not. This was not exactly what they had come for and there was only polite applause. I worked my way across the floor, blessing people as I went, to try to get to her, to say something to her. I finally reached her; she was surrounded by some reporters, and of course I couldn't speak. I would have given myself away. So I just looked at her. She had a beautiful face. She was Audrey Hepburn in *The Nun's Story* and I was Peter Finch. She was lovely, and I'm sorry, Judy, and I'm sorry, anybody else who might be offended, the girl being a nun and all, but I had just fallen instantly in love with her. I reached out for her hand, a silent mad-man wearing a veil and sunglasses. She took my hand in hers, in thanks, and this gentle girl smiled up at me. We were doomed as a couple—but it was a sweet moment.

The day's session ended and I was swept out onto the street by the crowd. I waited at the curb for the light to change next to where a little Good Humor man with a cart had set up. The Good Humor man was our Lord.

176

"Good God!" I said.

"Good Humor," He said.

"What are you doing here?"

"Selling the Flavor of the Week and listening in on the gossip."

"That outfit!" I said, pointing at His suit and cap.

"You look pretty nifty yourself."

"I didn't want to attract attention."

"It's some getup. This is my representative on earth?"

"I wanted to stay out of the headlines after I got your last note."

"You said it. What a nut that book fella was. I saw him on Johnny Carson."

"Then you're not mad at me?"

"God should hold personal grudges? And right now, you don't count so much anyway, if you excuse my saying. This conference is the thing. Terrific, huh? What a lot of religiousniks."

"Doesn't it bother you—the way they're sitting judgment?"

"So that's what they need to do. I think it's kind of fancy."

"Well, as you said, they've got the ball, let them run with it," looking to disavow responsibility.

"It's really something. This is big stuff."

I noticed that He had a little portable radio and He had been listening to the radio reports.

"If you want to know what's happening, couldn't you just absorb it, or however you know things?"

"This is better. A person comes out, he buys an ice-cream pop, he talks to another person on how it's going, and I listen to how it's going. Not just any Good Humor Man could do this. You got to be able to understand every language."

"What *is* going to happen here?"

"You're asking me?"

"You don't know?"

"How could I know?"

"You're God. You know everything."

"I know everything from before. I know everything from now. I don't know anything from what's going to be."

"You really don't know?"

"The future? Not a prayer."

"Not even what's going to happen tomorrow?"

"Not even what's going to happen for dinner."

"That's astounding."

"Why so? I know what is. How can I know what isn't?"

"I didn't realize you had any limitations."

"So write a paper on it. You can be a big philosopher, if you don't feel you're big enough."

"If you don't know, who does?"

"Nobody I know."

"When I first interviewed you and I asked you about the future of the planet, you said you didn't get into that—"

"I don't."

178

"But it never occurred to me that you really didn't know."

"Don't think I'm not interested."

"But if *you* don't even know where the world is headed—that's very disturbing."

"That's the way it is."

"But why did you come to us *now?* Why now? This must have been a warning. You must know something."

"I know everything. But not that."

"But is the world in a crisis? Is anything imminent?"

"Sure, you're in a crisis. Everything's imminent. You didn't know that?"

"I knew that."

"So everybody knows it. Look, it's a very important conference here. A lot of big shots. When it's over, if they say it was a miracle, there'll probably be a lot of 'What do we do nows?' and something will come of it."

I wanted to go racing into the hall to tell everybody I have God outside and He just said definitively that *He* doesn't even know if we're going to make it, so let's do something! Get together! Straighten out the world! Only dressed like a crazy Arab, babbling about a Good Humor man, they'd lock me up again.

"Where's that little French girl?" I said.

"French *nun* you mean."

"We can work on it together."

"You got a crush on her? I think you want to date her up."

"Would *you* talk to them?"

"I already did that, through you."

"But they don't all believe."

"That's their problem."

An English priest walked up and asked for a strawberry Good Humor.

"We're out of strawberry. How about chocolate chip?"

"Fine."

"How is it in there?" God asked.

"Very argumentative."

"Could I ask what you think?" He said. "Was a miracle? God was here?"

"Impossible. In my view, God would never appear in that manner or to that person."

"Well, I wouldn't know. I'm just the Good Humor man."

The priest turned to me. "What do you think, sir? Do you speak English?" I blessed him.

He walked away, eating his ice-cream pop. I spun at God.

"Now wait a minute. Wait just a minute. How did he see you? How did he talk to you? You said you appeared this way for me. If that's so, how did *he* see you?"

"He doesn't know I'm God."

"But he *saw* you!"

"That's right."

"Do you do this a lot?"

"What?"

"Just show up."

"Now and then. But nobody knows who I am."

"*Were* you at the Whalers' Festival?"

"So I happen to like cold beer and clams."

"God walks around and people don't even know it. Incredible! That man could *see* you!"

"You miss the point. He saw me as a Good Humor man. The trick is to know *that* Good Humor man is God."

"Look, something has to be done here. I've got to—"

"What? What can you do? I gave you The Word and you worked it all the way up to this high-class conference. That's good. We both did good. We're covered."

He opened the freezer. "Here, have an ice-cream pop and go home. Watch it on TV. You want chocolate chip, cherry jubilee, toasted almond?"

He handed me a pop.

"It's on the house. Don't say I never did nothing for you."

"Thank you."

"It's all right. Be careful you don't drip on your veil."

I turned to leave and just as I did, God moaned. He looked like He was in pain.

"What's the matter?" I said.

"Ten-year-olds in Indianapolis singing 'God Bless America.'"

The conference was nearing the end amid wild speculations as to the outcome. The delegates had agreed among themselves to act as sort of quasi-jurors and not tell outsiders how they would vote, so there were no valid straw polls of delegates. NBC programmed its computer for a computer-view of the possibility of a miracle and came up with a "too-close-to-call." Jimmy "the Greek" Snyder in Las Vegas took the miracle off the board—no bets—because he felt "you shouldn't bet on such a thing," prompting a big New York gambler to say bitterly, "Yeah, I bet the priests are dumping."

I was following the last two days at home, drinking mint tea and wearing the djellaba as a bathrobe. By now, all those behind-the-scenes committees were finally surfacing. The Miracles Committee gave a report to the delegates on the history and the evaluation requirements for miracles. The Opinion Committee synthesized the various opinions at the conference. The Evidence Committee gave a report on the evidence submitted, dismissing all evidence as hearsay, except for the findings of the Georgetown Group, which was given a special report by the Georgetown Group Committee. That committee said that the Georgetown Group, although distinguished, could not be considered representative of the world's spiritual leaders, owing to their exclusively American nationality, which to my mind didn't address itself to the question of a miracle at all, but my mind had its own committee, reporting on me and supplying, to my astonishment, evidence from an F.B.I. dossier characterizing me as "having the hint of a radical" about me and that I was "potentially pink" and an "incipient troublemaker." I was beginning to have

182

trouble focusing. Fortunately, the next report was from the Procedure Committee explaining the courses of action the conference could take: they could take no action and simply disband; they could leave it all for further exploration by a committee; or they could vote on whether or not a miracle had taken place. After a vote on whether to vote, they decided to vote.

The actual balloting would take place on the next and final day of the conference, giving the delegates overnight to search their consciences, pray, and consider the reports.

I couldn't sleep that night. I was up all night with a major anxiety attack. At one point in my nervousness I thought it would be nice if God would come by just to chat, but that's another thing He doesn't do.

The following morning, I was in front of my television set at 9 A.M. with a double Bloody Mary. The vote was to take place about an hour later and the networks filled time by running highlights of the previous sessions, by which time I had switched to straight vodka.

Finally, they were ready in the General Assembly. One of the chairman announced:

"Attention please. We shall commence the balloting. The question before the delegates is: 'As a spiritual leader, and a representative of your faith, based on your judgment of the evidence and the opinions presented at this ALLFAITH conference, do you believe a miracle has taken place and that God has appeared on earth at this time?' "

What a question. Two thousand people who weren't even there, voting on the opinions of other people who weren't there. But this was it. The hall became silent.

"All who vote *yes?*"

The delegates stood in their places and were counted.

"Three hundred thirty-two."

"All who vote *no?*"

"One thousand four hundred fifty-nine."

"Abstentions?"

"Two hundred eleven."

"The *no's* have it. A miracle has not taken place."

There was a roar, delegates cheering as though their man had just won an election, cheering as though a miracle *had* taken place. It was crazy. They didn't want to believe. It was just too much for them. Too threatening, too miraculous—I don't know. These experts had declared for all the world to know that God hadn't been there—and at that very moment He was sitting right outside the hall selling toasted almond.

On the floor, it was a madhouse. Those who voted *yes* were furious, those who voted *no* were furious at those who voted *yes*—there was yelling, some pushing and a couple of fistfights actually broke out. Fistfights! Spiritual people and punches were thrown. Someone at the platform yelled, "Let us pray" and the delegates found themselves again, although you could just sense the fury underneath. They went through a series of prayers closing the conference by each of the participating religions that lasted five hours, then the exhausted delegates adjourned and went home. They had done their job.

Judy tried to console me, but I was beyond reach and smashed on vodka. I watched the windup of the television coverage with my eyes closing, finally falling asleep in my chair. When I woke up, I needed a walk in the air by myself to clear my head. Outside it was getting dark now. No one was there but the man with the signs. Couldn't shake him.

I started to walk toward the U.N., which is a few blocks away, thinking about the conference and thinking about Him. When I first met Him, I wasn't sure He cared about us. But I'd begun to feel He did care. He watched us. He kept up with where we were. He even moved among us. What could He be thinking now? He had come here to reassure us that the world He created for us could work—and the world's religious leaders had voted against Him.

Near the U.N. there were all the signs of the aftermath of a convention. A few people were milling around, the streets were dirty with leaflets. At the corner, I saw Him. He was sitting hunched on a little stool next to the ice-cream cart. I went up to Him, but I didn't know what to say. I just shrugged. And He shrugged. He looked very disappointed, a lonely old man.

17

I DON'T want to make too much of a World Series analogy out of this, but the period after the ALLFAITH conference was like the time following a particularly exciting Series. What had for a few intense days dominated headlines and conversation, suddenly lost its hold. There were some postscripts, some follow-up features in the press and then a drop-off of interest.

Sales of *The Man Who Saw God* plummeted, an index of how successful the conference was in discrediting my story. Faithful as ever, F. X. Franckks sent me a note:

"My sweet person, I still believe in you and in God."

On the back of the envelope, he wrote something I haven't seen in years—S.W.A.K. "Sealed With A Kiss."

Religious leaders hurried to re-group and take a let's-get-back-to-business attitude—and it worked. Most people were content to go along with it—it was just easier to accept that the miracle never happened. Within two weeks of the conference, the business of religion was almost back to normal.

A Louis Harris Poll of the general public on whether or not God had appeared produced some believers: 6% Yes, against 43% No and 51% No Opinion. Among the clergy, there were a few holdouts, but they were greatly in the minority. A few anti-establishment breakaway religions popped up as well, but their philosophies were very vague, the most popular a non-denominational group called "The New Truth," big on communes, whose philosophy translated roughly as "anybody you meet could be God, so love thy neighbor, because you never know."

As far as public reaction to me personally was concerned, nothing was held against me. People didn't feel they had been hoaxed—just that I was a complete nut. Meantime, the God controversy, what was left of it, simply shifted away from me. I was finished in the media. I was yesterday's fruitcake.

Judy began making plans to get a job. I was waiting

for my next instructions from Him, but it was now three weeks since the conference ended and He was nowhere to be seen. I took to walking around the city to pass the time. You can't believe just how many little old messengers look like God when you're looking for Him.

One day, I called the house from a phone booth on Forty-second Street. The phone rang back and I picked it up.

"Hello, it's me, God."

"Hello! Where are you?"

"In the next booth."

There He was, standing right next to me on the phone, and looking much cheerier than when I saw Him last.

"Too many people around," He said. "It would be suspicious if somebody recognized you."

"They'd notice you first," I said.

He was wearing a safari hat, a bush jacket, jodhpurs and boots, none of which fit Him.

"I'm going on a little trip—to spend some time with animals. I like animals and sometimes I don't spend enough time."

"Are you all right? I was worried about you."

"You think God can't take care of Himself?"

"I wondered where you were."

"I don't have to account. The fact is I was making up my mind."

"And what should I do next?"

"Nothing."

186

"What do you mean?"

"I mean there's nothing to do. I came to say good-bye."

"Goodbye? Are you going just for now?"

"For now and for later."

"You're not coming back?"

"No. That's what I decided. I did what I came to do. It didn't work out as good as I wanted. But those who want to believe, so they'll believe—and the others, so they won't. I got a few people to think about things, though, that's pretty good."

He waved at me through the glass.

"So that's it. Take care, *bubeleh*. I'll be watching."

"But you can't go."

"It's time already."

"You can't—"

"It's time."

"But there are things I should be asking you."

"We did all that."

"And there must be things you want me to do—"

"No."

"There must be something."

"Well, you're a writer. Why don't you write about it?"

He was really going.

"It's too soon," I said.

"I think we got some pretty good business done."

"I don't mean only that. I was just getting to know you. I mean, our relationship was just beginning."

"These days, relationships are very difficult."

"Sometimes, now and then, couldn't we just talk?"

"I'll tell you what. *You* talk. *I'll* listen."

Then He threw me a little kiss and He walked away. He was gone. It was over just like that. I never saw Him again.

I've thought a lot since then about the whole experience and I thought it would be great if I could sum it up in one profound, magical paragraph that says it all. I couldn't. I tried to write it so many times, I lost count. The best I can offer on my feelings about Him is this:

I wish we could have gotten closer.